BREAKING PROTOCOL

FIREHOUSE FOURTEEN
BOOK 3

LISA B. KAMPS

Lisa B. Kamps

Breaking Protocol

Firehouse Fourteen
Book 3

Lisa B. Kamps

BREAKING PROTOCOL

Cover and logo design by Jay Aheer of Simply Defined Art
http://www.jayscoversbydesign.com/

Lisa B. Kamps

Lisa B. Kamps

DEDICATION

For Candice Davidson, Shawn-Leigh Wood, and Shelly Barca. Our paths may have changed but the connection remains the same! Can't wait to see you guys again on my next trip to SD!

BREAKING PROTOCOL

Contents

BREAKING PROTOCOL

Lisa B. Kamps

Other titles by this author

THE BALTIMORE BANNERS

Crossing The Line, Book 1
Game Over, Book 2
Blue Ribbon Summer, Book 3
Body Check, Book 4
Break Away, Book 5
Playmaker (A Baltimore Banners Intermission novella)
Delay of Game, Book 6
Shoot Out, Book 7
On Thin Ice, Book 8
The Baltimore Banners 1st Period Trilogy (Books 1-3)

FIREHOUSE FOURTEEN

Once Burned, Book 1
Playing With Fire, Book 2
Breaking Protocol, Book 3
Into The Flames, Book 4

STAND-ALONE TITLES

Emeralds and Gold: A Treasury of Irish Short Stories
(*anthology*)
Finding Dr. Right, Silhouette Special Edition
Time To Heal
Dangerous Heat

Lisa B. Kamps

Chapter One

Engines rumbled in the background, echoing off the hills surrounding them, bouncing back and destroying the silence of an otherwise still night. Spotlights illuminated the scene, casting everything in a harsh, unforgiving light.

Dave Warren adjusted his grip on the bag mask, walking backward as the engine crew carried the stokes basket down the hill. His foot tripped over a loose branch and he nearly slipped in the mud but somebody grabbed him by the belt and held him upright.

"Chopper's here waiting." Pete Miller shouted in his ear and Dave nodded before tossing a glance behind him. They had reached the stretcher and were transferring the patient onto it. The patient would be onboard the medevac in a matter of minutes, then on his way to Shock Trauma.

Dave didn't think it would really matter and was surprised they had even agreed to fly the patient out. Protocol stressed ten minutes on scene then gone, and the ETA for the chopper was rarely less than fifteen minutes.

But they had already been on scene for well over thirty minutes, trying to reach the remote area of the ATV accident in the dark, off a muddy, washed-out and little-used fire trail. It was anybody's guess how long the patient had been waiting before his friends had finally managed to get out and call 911.

Dave looked down at the patient again, at the misshapen skull and avulsed face, and realized again that it probably didn't matter what they did. It was just a matter of time before the teen died.

He looked up and surveyed the chaos around them, paying little attention to the flashing lights of the engines and medic, the harsh spotlights that turned night to day. His eyes searched for the source of the other noise he heard, a noise so familiar to him he still heard it in his sleep: the whirring motor and high-pitched wail of a waiting helicopter. A figure walked through the crowd, its silhouette dark and undefined until it moved closer.

Dave instructed his partner, Jimmy Hughes, to take over then straightened, waiting for the Flight Medic to get closer.

Then blinked as the silhouette moved closer and revealed itself.

The medic was small, petite, the top of her head just reaching his chest. And there was no doubt she was a she, not even under all the gear she was wearing: bulky flight suit, helmet, utility belt. Shoulder holster.

Dave blinked again, pushing his second-long observations to the back of his mind as the medic stopped next to him and looked up.

"What do you have?" Her voice was loud and clear, each word enunciated to be heard over the chaos around them, filled with authority despite the casual, slightly accented words.

"Nineteen-year old male, ATV accident. Looks like he flew head-first into a tree. No helmet. Unresponsive." Dave rattled off the list of other injuries with the detachment of someone reading a grocery list. The medic took notes, nodding to indicate she heard.

"Tubed?"

"Getting there."

"Alright, let's get him loaded, we can do it onboard." She tucked the pad into a bulky pocket on the side of her leg then turned back to Dave. "You the paramedic?"

"Yeah."

"Okay Big Guy, you're with me. We're flying an old one tonight. Let's go." She motioned toward the waiting helicopter then turned to the engine crew and issued instructions in her clear voice.

The patient was quickly loaded and Dave was ready to climb into the waiting chopper when a strong hand stopped him. He turned to look down, surprised at the strength in the small woman's hand.

"Have you flown before?" She shouted the question to be heard above the whirl of the blades overhead. Dave tried not to look insulted.

"Yeah, I've flown before."

"Didn't meant to upset you, Big Guy, just had to ask. We don't do this much anymore." She motioned for him to climb in, then jumped in after him and handed him a headset. He dropped it over his ears and pulled the mike in front of his mouth, his attention focused solely on the patient in front of him as the helicopter engine whirred to full life and lifted off, leaving the chaos beneath them.

They had the patient intubated and fluids running, doing what they could to keep the kid with them by the time the helicopter landed at Shock Trauma fifteen minutes later. A trauma team was already waiting for them and Dave was pushed out of the way as someone in pink scrubs took over the patient's breathing. He followed the team inside and down the hallway, into a waiting trauma room.

He peeled off his bloody gloves and tossed them into the biohazard waste can, then stood off to the side and watched as the team of trauma specialists took over, each move synchronized, as if it had been rehearsed and carefully choreographed.

"We're losing him. Someone crack his chest. CC, get up here and squeeze."

Dave watched as a line was cut down the patient's breastbone, as his ribs were spread apart, opening his insides to the world. The Flight Medic jumped on a small step stool and reached in with one small hand, a look of concentration on her face as she squeezed the patient's heart with her hand.

Twenty minutes elapsed before the lead surgeon shook his head and called it, pronouncing time of death at zero one thirty-two. A momentary hush settled over the room, then the team began the process of cleaning up so the body could be moved to the morgue.

Dave stepped out of the way, his mind already focused on finding a quiet spot so he could call the EMS Supervisor and make sure he had a ride back to the station. The Flight Medic turned, her expression displaying her surprise to find him still standing there.

"Hey Big Guy, didn't realize you were still here." She stopped next to him and removed her gloves with a snap before tossing them into the bio-waste can. She nudged him out of the way then washed her hands at the sink, her movements concise and economical.

"Dave."

"What's that?" She wadded up the paper towels she had used to dry her hands and tossed them into the trash can, her clear hazel eyes never leaving his.

"My name is Dave Warren. Not Big Guy."

She raised one finely arched blonde brow in his direction then finally nodded, the motion barely perceptible. Dave had the distinct impression that she didn't give a rat's ass what his name was.

The thought didn't amuse him, and he didn't know why.

"And your name would be?"

She looked up at him again, her full mouth tilted at one corner. "Are you asking for you, or your report?"

Dave narrowed his eyes. "My report."

"In that case, it's Covey. C. Covey."

He nodded, still studying her. "And if it wasn't for my report?"

"Then it's CC."

"And that's spelled—?"

She laughed, the sound clear and refreshing, completely incongruous in the bloody mayhem surrounding them. "Capital C. Capital C. CC."

He frowned at her, wondering if stress and lack of sleep had finally addled his brain to the point where he was having trouble understanding simple English. She laughed again, then turned and started walking away. She paused, then looked back over her shoulder at him.

"I'm getting a coffee. Would you like some?"

Dave paused, surprised at the invitation. Surprised even more that he wanted to say yes. So he merely nodded then followed the petite woman down the hallway to the small break room.

"To answer the question you think is too impolite to ask, they're my initials. CC. Carolann Covey." She laughed at his expression, the sound almost music to his tired ears. She poured coffee, black, into a small Styrofoam cup then grabbed one of the small mismatched plastic chairs and turned it around. She swung her leg over one side and sat, straddling the chair backwards as she smiled at him. "Yes, I'm from down South, and no, my momma and daddy didn't want me to be a stripper, despite the name."

Dave poured his own black coffee and leaned against the counter, wondering if the thick drawl was deliberate, then wondering why she would bother. He didn't say anything, didn't even know how to respond to her comment. She laughed again and gave him a small wink.

"And aren't you the polite one, not saying a word about it."

"No. I, uh—"

"Don't worry about it." She waved him off with a small motion of her hand, then took a sip of the coffee. Dave was surprised that she didn't even grimace at the bitterness. "So tell me, Mr. Paramedic Dave Warren, was that your first cracked chest?"

Whatever Dave had been expecting for conversation, if he even had been, it wasn't that. He fixed the small woman looking up at him with a steady gaze, then shook his head. "No. I've seen it done before, once or twice."

She nodded and took another sip of the coffee. "Hm. Why am I thinking that you've seen a lot more, and that it wasn't here?" She kept studying him with those clear eyes that seemed to see deep below the surface. He looked away, suddenly uncomfortable, afraid she would see too much.

And find him falling short.

But she said nothing, just murmured another noncommittal "Hm" and drank her coffee.

Dave's phone vibrated against his belt and he unclipped it to see a text message from the EMS Supervisor on the screen, letting him know to meet downstairs in five minutes. Dave clipped the phone back to his belt and drained the coffee. He looked up and noticed that the medic—that CC—was already tossing her crushed cup into the trashcan and was heading out the door. She paused in the doorway and turned back to him, a smile on her full lips.

"See? We already have two things in common."

He blinked, not sure he understood. "Pardon?"

"We both drink black coffee. And I'm pretty sure we both spent some time playing in the sandbox. See you around, Big Guy." She gave him another playful wink then disappeared down the hallway, leaving him to wonder what had just happened.

It wasn't until he was halfway back to the station that her parting words finally clicked, and he understood just what she had meant.

Then he wondered what she had seen that made her realize he had spent time in hell.

Chapter Two

CC rapped her knuckles against the door for the second time, wondering if anyone was home, or if she was just wasting her time. A truck sat in the driveway, an impressive full-size extended cab heavy duty job. Shiny black paint, shiny chrome. The truck fit the owner, she thought.

If it actually belonged to Big Guy.

She stepped back from the door and looked around. The neighborhood was quiet, the homes on the upper end of modest and nicely maintained. The lawn that spread out around her was neatly clipped and edged, the flower beds that lined the walk from the driveway filled with blooming bushes and a selection of vibrantly colored flowers. She had no idea what kind of flowers, knew only that they looked nice.

She glanced at her watch. It wasn't quite ten o'clock in the morning. Maybe the Big Guy was in the shower. Or maybe he wasn't even home.

Or maybe he was sleeping.

CC smiled at the clear visual that sprung to mind,

immediately figuring him for a guy who slept in the buff. And wouldn't that be a nice little treat, if he answered the door like that?

Figuring the third time was a charm, she opened the screen once more and rapped her knuckles against the thick wood door. Harder this time, just in case.

Maybe a little too hard, since she could hear muffled grumbling coming from the other side. The door finally opened, only about six inches, but wide enough for her to realize that the Big Guy had, indeed, been sleeping.

Unfortunately, not in the buff.

But damn close to it.

Her eyes raked over his body in slow appreciation, from his sleep-mussed black hair and piercing chocolate eyes, down to his broad well-defined chest. And wasn't she the lucky one, because that chest was deliciously bare. Her eyes continued their slow descent, down past his sculpted abs and lean hips—damn shame he was wearing such baggy shorts—to his strong legs and bare feet.

Her eyes reversed their travel, pausing to study the intricately drawn tattoo on his left chest, and came back to rest on his dark eyes. She didn't miss the scowl on his face, an expression that made him look just like a pirate, especially with the dark stubble that shadowed his strong chin and jaw.

"Can I help you?" His voice was gruff, hoarse with sleep. Not a single flicker of recognition showed in his eyes.

CC slid the sunglasses up to her head, anchoring them in her hair, and gave him a big smile.

"Hey Big Guy. Did I wake you?"

Recognition, and something very much like

surprise, quickly registered on his face. He stepped back, but didn't open the door any wider or invite her in.

"You!"

"Yup, it's me. So, you going to invite me in?" She reached her hand out and nudged the door open a bit, her eyes quickly roaming around the shadowed interior. Neutral living room with a dining room just beyond, stairs leading up off to the right. "Or are you hiding a wife or girlfriend in here?"

He stepped back in mute surprise as she walked past him. He wasn't married—she had already checked on that—but she wasn't sure about the girlfriend part. She looked over her shoulder at him, not surprised that he hadn't moved.

"What?" His brows pulled down in an angry slash as he stared at her. "No! To either one."

"Hey, just checking. Sometimes you can never tell so better safe than sorry."

"No." He shook his head, then turned back to the door and looked surprised that it was still standing open. He closed it, probably harder than he intended, then turned back to face her. He ran both hands across his face then up through his hair and exhaled deeply. "Is there a reason you're here?"

"Yeah. I found this in the chopper, thought you might want it back." She pulled his wallet from the back pocket of her jeans and tossed it to him. It hit him dead center in the chest and he reached up, fumbling to catch it before it hit the ground. He stared at it for a long second, then shook his head again.

"My wallet. Yeah, I know. I was going to run down later today to pick it up at the barracks."

"Lucky you. I just saved you a trip." She walked

into the living room and looked around, her eyes taking in more details. Not that there was much to see.

A beige leather sofa and loveseat formed an L, allowing optimal viewing of the large screen television mounted to the far wall. Matching dark oak end tables flanked the sofa, complementing the dark oak coffee table placed conveniently in the middle of the arrangement. Boring. Really boring. A few pictures on the wall added some color, as did the area rug. Other than that, there wasn't much to see.

She moved through the living room to the dining room. A shaker style oak table with whitewashed legs was flanked by four ladder back chairs and a matching bench. An old fashioned hutch stood to the side, an assortment of dishes and collectibles stacked behind the glass doors.

The furniture and decoration wasn't bad, but she would have preferred some color herself.

"So. Do you have anything to drink around here, Big Guy?" He was right behind her, she could feel his presence less than a foot away, and she didn't have to turn around to know he was still scowling. She bit back her smile and wandered into the kitchen, knowing he was following her.

Now this was more like it, she thought. The kitchen was bright and airy, with big windows and French doors opening to the backyard. Yellows, greens and blues mixed in a vibrant color scheme, an extension of the outdoors contained just beyond the glass. She moved over to the counter island, hooked the heel of her boot around a stool, and pulled it out. She sat her elbows on the granite surface, propped her chin in her hands, and offered Big Guy a bright smile.

He was still scowling at her, confusion warring

with something else on his face. One hand reached up and he absently scratched at his chest, pulling her attention once again to the tattoo.

About five inches square, it was a detailed black ink drawing of a caduceus against a tattered Flag. The words "My Brother's Keeper" formed a border along the top and side. Even from this distance, she could see the detail was exquisite, and her fingers itched to trace the lines.

And not just of the tattoo.

"Nice ink. When'd you get it?"

"Excuse me?" He glanced down at his chest, then dropped his hand to the side, his fingers curling into a loose fist. She could feel his frustration from where she sat, and smiled even wider. "I'm sorry, but is there a reason you're here?"

"Just wanted to drop off your wallet."

"And you did, thank you. Now you can leave."

CC didn't flinch at his rudeness, not when she knew it was a result of his being flustered, by not knowing what to make of her. She almost laughed, but didn't think he'd appreciate it. "You can't even offer me a drink before I go? I'm not picky. Water's fine."

Big Guy watched her with narrowed eyes, his impatience and uncertainty warring with something else, something that caused just a brief flicker of heat to flash in his dark eyes. He muttered something then turned his back on her and reached up to grab a glass from a cabinet. Her eyes roamed across his broad shoulders and down his back, down to the tight ass that even his baggy shorts couldn't hide.

He turned on the faucet and let it run for a second, then placed the glass under the running water until it was filled. He brought the glass over and sat it in front of her with a small clink, his gaze still narrowed.

"No ice?"

Without a word, he turned to the steel-fronted refrigerator, opened the door, and reached into the ice bin. He returned and plunked two ice cubes into the glass, ignoring the water that splashed over the rim.

"Thank you." She smiled and raised the glass in a mock salute then took a long swallow, her eyes never leaving his. She lowered the glass and ran her tongue across her lips, noticing that his gaze dropped to her mouth, watching. Another flare of heat sparked in his eyes and he looked away.

"Now that you've dropped off my wallet—and had something to drink—you can leave now."

"Are you always so grumpy, Big Guy?"

"Dave. The name is Dave." He uttered the words through clenched teeth, his frustration clear. "And when strangers show up at my house uninvited, yes, I get a little grumpy."

"Strangers, hm?" She took another swallow of water then put the glass down, pushing it out of her way. She folded her arms on the counter then leaned forward, watching him. "You know, something funny about that. I've learned that people who talk to one another, get to know each other, aren't strangers for very long."

Dave just watched her, saying nothing. She kept her eyes on his, refusing to look away. A small twitch teased the corner of his mouth, just the briefest movement, but she saw it. Saw it, and smiled.

His tension eased out of him, bit by bit until his shoulders weren't hunched quite so tightly against his ears. Lines eased from his face, relaxing his mouth and eyes and making him look younger, less worried, more approachable. CC felt a small glimmer of victory shoot through her at the transformation. She knew she hadn't read him wrong last night.

"That's really nice work, by the way." She nodded her head to the tattoo again. "When did you get it done?"

He looked down at his chest then up at her and shrugged. "About three years ago. Um, excuse me, I need to go grab a shirt—"

"No, really, you don't. I'm kind of enjoying the scenery." Her words stopped him cold and he froze mid-step, the tips of his ears turning pink. She watched the muscles in his strong throat work, and briefly wondered if he was trying to swallow—or trying not to choke. He didn't say anything but he did turn to look at her, now only a foot away from her.

She swiveled on the stool and leaned forward, reaching out and tracing the outline of the tattoo with the tip of her finger. The muscle underneath was rock hard, the flesh firm and hot, scorching. His chest rose and fell with one deep breath before his hand shot out and closed around her wrist.

She slid off the stool and stepped next to him, looking up into his eyes, watching heat swirl in their depths.

"What are you doing?" His voice was a hoarse whisper, tugging at something deep inside her. But there was something else, a wariness, a hunger, a deep need that pulsed through him and into her.

"So I'm not the only one who felt it." She breathed the words, barely aware of saying them out loud, wondering even as she said them what he was thinking.

What would he think if she leaned up and pressed her lips against the pulse beating heavily at the base of his throat? If she leaned up and pressed her lips against his mouth?

Anticipation, excitement, need. Heat. Desire. They swirled together, building, mixing with something else, something basic and primitive that pulled them closer.

Fire flamed in the depths of his eyes and her body burned from the heat of his skin, so close. His hand tightened around her wrist and she saw the hesitation, the confusion on his face. She thought he'd step back or push her away.

Then his mouth crashed against hers, hot, hungry, demanding. She moaned as his tongue plunged into the recesses of her mouth, searching with greedy need. His hand released her wrist and she flattened her palm against his chest, against hard muscle and hot flesh.

His arms came around her waist and pulled her closer, his hands cupping her ass and molding her hips against his body. Another moan escaped her as he pressed the rigid length of his erection against her stomach, rocking against her with a throaty growl she felt clear down to the tips of her toes.

Her hands drifted up to his shoulders, wrapping around his neck. She brushed her fingers through the short strands of his hair, surprised at the softness.

He deepened the kiss, the pounding in his chest matching the throbbing in her veins. She leaned in closer, needing to feel more of him, all of him, needing to lose herself.

He dragged his hand up her back, his calloused palm skimming the flesh as he dragged the hem of her shirt up. His touch was hot, searing, and she moaned again at the sensation, the sound lost in their kiss.

And then he pulled away with a ragged groan, his

breathing harsh, heavy. Hooded eyes stared down at her, dazed. He blinked. Looked at her and blinked again.

He pulled his hands away from her body and stepped back, an expression of horror crossing his face before he looked away. Disappointment raced through her as she watched him run his hands over his face, his chest rising and falling with each harsh breath.

She reached behind her, searching for the stool, then slid onto it, a smile lifting her lips when he finally looked at her.

"Jesus Christ. Are you insane?"

She pretended to think about it, then shook her head. "No."

"Really? So you make it a habit of just showing up at some guy's—some *stranger's* house and...and..." He waved his hand between them, unable to finish his sentence. She watched him again, her lips pursed in thought. Then she shook her head.

"Nope, can't say I do. This is pretty much a new one for me."

He ran both hands through his hair, mussing the short length even more, then folded his hands behind his neck and looked up at the ceiling, his lips forming around silent words. CC grabbed the glass of water and took a sip, watching him.

"Why are you here? And don't tell me it was to return my wallet."

She shrugged and put the glass down. "You intrigued me."

"Intrigued? I intrigued you? So you show up at my house and try—" He waved his hand between them again. For some reason, his discomfort and confusion amused her and she laughed. His eyes narrowed and he stepped away, reaching down to adjust himself. She didn't even think he realized he did it, which only made her smile more.

"And what the hell would you have done if I hadn't stopped?"

She lowered her gaze pointedly, then looked back up and met his eyes. "Well. I'm hoping I would have enjoyed it. A lot."

He groaned, a sound of frustration, then muttered under his breath before exhaling. "You need to leave. Please."

CC let her eyes wander the length of his body once more before sliding off the stool with a smile. She reached into her back pocket and pulled out a small card, then moved to stand to next to him. She ran the edge of the card down his chest, smiling when his breath hitched. Her other hand reached down and pulled out the waistband of his shorts, just enough so she could slide the card inside. She snapped his waistband back into place, patted it with her hand, then stepped away.

"Give me a call later if you want." She smiled again, then turned and made her way to the front door. She didn't have to look to know that his eyes were following her progress, because the heat of his gaze was burning the center of her back.

She smiled again as she pulled the door closed behind her, wondering how long it would take the serious man to unbend long enough to call her.

If he'd call her at all.

Chapter Three

Dave stared at the closed door for long minutes, his heart pounding in his chest.

"Jesus Christ."

What the hell had just happened? His side burned, seared from the touch of her small hand. Hell, his entire body still burned from the feel of her body pressed tight against him. The kiss replayed in his mind, hot, relentless.

He closed his eyes and took a deep breath, trying to force the image of the woman from his mind, trying to erase the phantom feel of her touch from memory. He reached down and pulled the card from the waistband of his shorts and looked down at it.

Trooper First Class C. Covey

Flight Medic

Below that was the name of the barracks, address, and contact information.

And on the back, written in a tiny neat hand, was a cell phone number.

Dave stared at the business card for a long minute,

then tossed it on the coffee table and turned toward the stairs. He had no time for even thinking of something as brief as an affair, no matter how exciting he was sure it would be.

Jesus.

So why was he still thinking about it?

Jesus.

He paused outside Angie's old room, the walls still decorated with the few things she hadn't taken when she moved out a few months ago, but otherwise empty. He knew his sister was doing fine, knew because he saw her damned boyfriend each day at work.

Just one more thing he didn't want to think about right now, the rift between his sister and him.

Because he had been acting like an ass for the past eight months.

He turned into the spare bedroom, seeking an outlet for the frustration running through him. Frustration from work, frustration from his estrangement with Angie.

And now, the sexual frustration from CC's brief visit.

He spent two hours with the weights, working until sweat poured from his body and each muscle ached with fatigue. Yet the frustration stuck with him, unrelenting. Frustration, and something else.

Stress. Worry.

He sat on the bench, his head in his hands, his breath coming in short gasps. His phone beeped, a set of three shrill chirps, and he stood up to retrieve it from the side table.

He looked down at the text message and his gut twisted with guilt and rage.

I know what you did.

In a sudden fit of temper, he threw the phone against the wall, where it hit then shot back, sliding across the hardwood floor. The screen shattered and bits of the plastic case broke off, bouncing up to hit him. A stinging sensation bit his chest and he looked down. A trickle of blood oozed from his left chest, the deep red marring the ink of the tattoo.

My Brother's Keeper.

Dammit.

It had been nearly four months since he had last received one of the cryptic messages, just days after Angie moved out. Four months of silence, of freedom, of thinking that whoever was behind the harassment had moved on.

Until last week, when they started again.

Cryptic, anonymous. Harassing and vaguely threatening. The messages all carried the same underlying meaning, the sender accusing Dave of something.

And he had no idea what they meant.

He had changed his number twice already, thinking that would help. But the messages still came.

I know what you did.

How do live with yourself?

You'll pay.

Your family will pay like mine paid.

It was that last message that had nearly pushed him over the edge, making him want to shelter and protect his kid sister. Making him push too hard and too far, so far she had actually moved out.

But she was safe, he knew. Safe and happy.

Please God, let her be safe.

He had ignored the messages at first, thinking someone was playing jokes. But as their frequency increased, so did his worry. His first thought was that they were from some nameless family member of a patient who may have died on one of their many calls. He had asked one of his cop friends to look into it quietly, but to no avail. The messages were sent anonymously, through a pay-as-you-go phone service from a disposable phone.

Virtually untraceable.

So he had changed his number and looked into every call he had been on, going back more than six months. Hundreds of calls, hundreds of patients.

And nothing stood out, nothing that could possibly prompt someone to send the threatening messages.

And then, four months ago, he received another one. Two words that froze the blood in his veins.

Helmand Province.

More than two years had gone by since he returned from his deployment. More than half of his eighteen months had been spent in that hell hole, and his time there as a medic in the Reserves still woke him up in the middle of some nights.

My Brother's Keeper.

He glanced down at the tattoo, frowning at the dried blood covering it. He had tried. They had all tried. Saved as many as they could, patched them up and got them out as fast as they could, hoping it would be enough.

Knowing that many times it wasn't.

And he lost a piece of himself with each soldier, with each Marine, that didn't make it.

My Brother's Keeper.

He wanted to believe it. But even he knew that sometimes, not even his best was good enough.

And somebody else knew it, too.

A chill swept over him, causing the skin of his arms and chest to raise in bumps as a prickle crept down his spine. He told himself there was nothing he could do, not now, not anymore.

And there was nothing the police could do.

The only thing he could do right now was get a new phone and change his number. Again. Hope that whoever was behind the messages would just give up. Then try to move on with his life, like everyone else that had been over there.

That was still over there.

He stepped over the shattered phone on his way to the shower, thinking he hadn't done a very good job of living in the last eight months.

The sight of clear hazel eyes and the sound of crystal laughter suddenly came to mind, unbidden. Carolann Covey, who hadn't been raised a stripper.

The corner of his mouth tilted in something that might vaguely resemble a smile, if anyone had been there to see it. He didn't want to think about the spitfire he had just met, didn't want to relive her visit this morning.

But now that her image was firmly in his mind, he couldn't get rid of it. And he knew, unequivocally and intuitively, that there was a woman who knew how to grab life by the throat and live it.

**

CC was dying.

The bubble rose past her face, distorted in the sun-dappled green water. It tickled her nose and her eyes as she watched its slow rise to the surface, expanding as it went higher, higher.

Another bubble burst from her lips, following the first one. And again she watched it, counting as the pressure grew in her lungs, burning, until she wanted to do nothing more than open her mouth and breathe in heaving gulps of air.

Which would be kind of a stupid thing to do, considering she was at the bottom of the cove, about fifteen feet from the surface. She dug her fingers deeper into her left calf, pressing harder, digging and digging, until the cramp finally released its death grip on what was left of the muscle.

Lights blinked behind her eyes, the colored starbursts looking like fireworks. She shook her head.

Easy, CC. Easy.

She pushed off with her right foot and shot to the surface, her lungs exploding, her mouth opening and sucking in huge gulps of air. She brushed the hair from her face, treading water as she turned her head, looking for the pier. One more deep breath then she turned to her side and kicked, her strong arms slicing through the water, dragging her useless left leg behind her.

Her hands closed around the rungs of the ladder and she pulled herself up, one hand over the other, bracing her weight with her right leg. She reached the sun-warmed planks of the pier and rolled over onto her back, her legs hanging off the edge as her chest rose and fell with each gasping breath.

One of these days, she was going to end up killing herself.

She pushed herself away from the edge and closed her eyes. The late afternoon sun was warm against her skin, drying the last of the water from her flesh. The cool September breeze brushed over her, its chill a refreshing contrast to the warmth of the sun.

Long minutes went by and she did nothing but relax, enjoying the feel of the sun and breeze against her skin as her breathing slowed. She took one last deep breath then pushed up on her elbows, squinting against the sun dropping to the horizon. She sat up, then bent at the waist and leaned forward, stretching her hands toward her toes.

The muscles in the backs of her legs stretched and pulled, her left calf burning. She wrapped her hand around the calf and worked the tips of her fingers into the knotted scar tissue, rubbing the mangled flesh until the last twinge of cramp finally disappeared.

She leaned back on her elbows again and watched the sun sink lower, peace filling her. Too many people rushed through each day, never slowing down, never stopping to relax and appreciate the world spinning around them.

She had been like that herself, not too long ago. A smile stretched across her face. Nothing like a life-altering experience to change your outlook.

She pushed to her feet and headed back to the house, the wood of the planks beneath her feet rough yet comforting. The slight rumbling in her stomach told her it was dinner time, and she did a mental rundown of potential menu items.

Maybe she'd grill some chicken and make a nice Caesar salad. Pasta to go with it? No, that would be too much food. A nice white wine.

And to finish it off, something chocolate. It didn't matter what, and she certainly had plenty to choose from. So she'd decide later, surprise herself.

She climbed the steps to the screened-in porch, holding the door so it wouldn't slam behind her, then moved through the other door that led to the back of the house. The cottage was small but comfortable, with two bedrooms, a living room and small dining room, nice kitchen. But it was the back porch she loved the most, and it was the first thing she had renovated and decorated when she bought the place a few years ago.

In fact, besides the waterfront view, the back porch was the other reason she had bought the place. It was her personal escape, filled with overstuffed wicker furniture, bright colors, and lots of green plants—plastic, so she couldn't kill them. The porch was where she spent most of her time when she was home, and what made the purchase worth every penny.

She still didn't know how she had lucked out in finding this place. Finding—and buying. It had to have been meant to be. She had decided to make the leap into home ownership but hadn't really decided where she wanted to live. A week later, someone at work had mentioned this place, located down a narrow road in an isolated area on the eastern side of the county, right on the water. And the price had been just right, actually lower than what she had been willing to spend.

It had been one of the best decisions she had ever made.

She pulled the container of chicken breasts from the refrigerator and pulled one out, then set about preparing it for the grill with a mix of seasonings and olive oil. She grabbed the romaine lettuce and chopped it, tossing it into a bowl with fresh parmesan cheese—straight from a bag, thank you—and salad dressing. She added a few croutons then placed the bowl in the refrigerator to chill.

She hesitated before grabbing the bottle of wine, then filled a glass with some of the sweet Riesling before taking the chicken out to the grill.

The chicken was done by the time she finished the wine, and she was sitting at the wicker table on the back porch with another glass, eating dinner fifteen minutes later.

The sun was nearly below the horizon now, the air just a bit chillier with the hint of fall. She'd take a shower, she decided, then dress in her most comfortable worn-out sweats and indulge in some chocolate brownie ice cream before bed.

Not the most exciting night to some, she was sure, but sometimes staying in was just what she needed.

She cut through her bedroom, stopping to grab her sweats and t-shirt, then headed to the bathroom. She had just reached into the shower, ready to turn on the water, when she heard the faint ring of her cell phone. Should she answer it and risk something interrupting her plans for the rest of the night? Yeah, she probably should. The chance of it being something important, someone important, was slim, but she didn't want to take the chance. Just in case.

Now all she had to do was find it.

She stopped in the middle of the bedroom, her head tilted to the side, listening. The ring sounded like it was coming from in here but the noise was muffled.

Where had she thrown it this time? If she didn't find it soon, she wouldn't have to worry about it because whoever was would just hang up.

Nope, there it was, hidden under a pile of clothes on the lone stuffed chair in the corner. She had no idea how it got there, couldn't even remember tossing it there. She threw the clothes to the side and grabbed it, answering it without looking down at the screen. "'Lo?"

Silence greeted her, a short pause followed by the soft sound of a clearing throat. Perfect. Probably a telemarketer, using one of those annoying robo calls. She was ready to disconnect the call, but was stopped when the voice on the other end finally spoke.

"Hey, it's Dave." Another pause. "Dave Warren."

A smile curled the corners of her mouth and she moved over to the bed, sitting down on the edge. "Hey Big Guy. What's up?"

"Nothing." His voice was gruff, his answer given almost grudgingly, like he had called against his will or better judgment. She smiled into the phone but didn't say anything. If he had taken the time to call, she certainly wasn't going to lead the conversation.

But several long seconds went by and she was beginning to wonder if he would actually say anything else. She was ready to take pity on him when the sound of a deep breath came across the phone, along with the visual of him running a hand through that thick shock of black hair.

"I was wondering if you wanted to grab a bite to eat." Again, his voice was rough, uncertain.

"Oh. Sorry, but I just ate."

"Oh. That's okay, maybe another time."

CC straightened on the bed, no longer smiling. Because she knew, *knew*, that he was going to hang up. And that it would be a long time before he called her again. If he ever called her again.

"But I haven't had dessert yet."

A long pause. "Dessert?"

She could only imagine what he was thinking, after this morning's visit, and laughed. "Don't worry, I mean real dessert. Like chocolate. It's one of the four major food groups."

Something that sounded like a chuckle, an honest-to-goodness almost-real chuckle, tickled her ear. Rusty, a little forced, and probably definitely unexpected as far as the speaker was concerned. CC smiled to herself. Progress, she thought.

"I think I can do chocolate."

"You mean there's people who can't? The horror!" Another chuckle? Or maybe just a cough disguised as a wheeze? CC closed her eyes, imagining dark chocolate eyes crinkling at the corners, a full sensuous mouth tilting up ever so slightly. How much more devastatingly handsome would he be if she ever actually got him to smile?

Then she snapped her eyes open and looked down at the ragged shorts and tank shirt she had been wearing all day, that she had been swimming in. She rolled her eyes and hurried into the bathroom, reaching in to turn on the water for the shower.

"What's that?"

"Hm? Oh, probably the shower, I'm getting ready to jump in."

There was another pause, another sound like he was clearing his throat.

Or possibly choking.

She put the phone on speaker then placed it on the counter, peeling off clothes as she spoke. "Do you know where the Thunderbird is, on Old Eastern Avenue?"

"Isn't that an ice cream place?"

"Ice cream, chocolate malts, and the absolute best hot fudge sauce this side of heaven. Meet in a half hour?"

There was another pause, shorter this time, and she imagined him glancing at his watch. "How about forty-five?"

"Even better. See you in a little bit, Big Guy." She hit the end button, cutting him off before he could remind her again that his name was Dave.

She smiled and climbed under the streaming water.

Yes, sometimes staying home was just what she needed.

And sometimes, it wasn't.

Chapter Four

Dave pulled into the parking lot, his eyes widening at the unexpected crowd. Dozens of cars filled the small lot and he searched for an open space. He hadn't expected this many people. To be honest, he hadn't really expected any people at all. It was a weeknight, the heat of summer was all but gone, and he didn't really think there was this much demand for ice cream.

Even if they did have the best hot fudge sauce this side of heaven.

He shook his head at the memory of her words, wrapped in that light accent of hers. He didn't know if it was all authentic, or slightly exaggerated for his benefit. All he knew was that the sound of her clear voice, almost musical, combined with an image of her standing naked while she talked to him had a completely unexpected effect on his body.

Yeah, so unexpected that his own shower had been very short, and very, very cold.

He pulled into an open spot in a dark corner of the lot then got out and locked the truck behind him, stopping to look around. It had been forty-five minutes exactly since he had gotten off the phone with CC, but he hadn't thought to ask where to meet her.

Hadn't realized he would have needed to. He looked around again then headed toward the building, thinking he'd find her out front.

The ice cream place was nothing more than a low, rectangular white building. It didn't offer indoor seating but it did have a few tables, chairs, and benches available outside. The building boasted two large sliding windows: one for placing your order and paying, the other for picking it up.

Quick, efficient, and—from the looks of the lines—extremely popular.

"Hey Big Guy."

Dave paused mid-step when he heard that clear voice calling him. He knew he should be surprised that he recognized not only the voice, but the name she called him as well.

But he wasn't.

And that worried him, because he had only just met her last night.

Had it really been just last night? Why did it seem so much longer?

He pushed the question from his mind then turned, his eyes drifting around the parking lot, searching her out. His gaze brushed over the woman leaning against a motorcycle, then sped back.

And sure enough, it was CC, her denim-clad legs crossed in front of her as she leaned against a sparkling Harley Fat Boy. He had a second's amazement that someone so petite could manage such a machine.

Then he had an image of her straddling the machine, controlling it as the powerful engine throbbed between her legs.

Dave had no idea what the hell was wrong with him, only knew that he needed to snap out of it. There were too many other things going on in his life right now, too many other worries, not the least of which were the recurring messages he was receiving.

So then why was he even here? What had prompted him to call CC in the first place?

It had been a whim, brought on by something needier within him, something he wasn't ready to admit to, something he wasn't willing to examine. But he was here now.

And so was she.

She was still leaning against the bike, watching him. Her blonde hair was longer than he had first realized, cascading almost to the middle of her back in loose waves. Her jeans were worn and faded, the denim molding to the generous curves of her hips and thighs before flaring slightly to cover the tops of worn black riding boots.

She was wearing a fitted long sleeve shirt, the v-cut just deep enough to reveal a generous swell of full, rounded breasts. A flash of warmth went through him at the memory of that feminine body and all its curves pressed against him this morning. But instead of making him smile, he scowled and again wondered what he was doing here.

CC's sudden laugh caught him by surprise and he almost stepped back, not sure why she was laughing. She pushed away from the bike and walked over to him, not stopping until she was close enough to run her hand across his chest with a little smile.

He was surprised that he stood still long enough to allow the familiarity.

But not surprised at the heat that danced along his flesh at the touch.

"Do you ever smile, Big Guy? Or is this grumpiness a permanent state for you?"

"I'm not grumpy."

"Hm." She looked up at him, her hazel eyes more green than brown in the reflection of the light that fell around them, and smiled. "Well, you may want to work on letting your face know, because that scowl sure says grumpy to me."

Dave looked down at her, not knowing how to respond. What could he say? He knew how to smile. He even knew how to laugh, dammit. He just hadn't done much of either lately. And it wasn't like he was going to tell her why, either.

But he didn't get a chance to say anything, anyway, because she suddenly grabbed his hand and pulled him toward the building, stopping when they reached the end of the line.

And she didn't let go of his hand.

He was surprised at the feel of her hand in his. Her fingers were long and slender, the bones almost fragile in his larger grip. But there was strength there, too, just beneath the surface. He glanced down, surprised at the strong physical differences between them. Small to his large; delicate to his rough; pale to his dark.

But despite the differences, he suddenly realized that anyone who underestimated this woman, did so at their own risk. It was a warning he would do well to remember, he thought.

CC suddenly raised their joined hands between them, a grin on her face.

"You okay with this, Big Guy? Or does it bother you?"

"Uh, no." He cleared his throat and looked down, mortified to feel his face heat under her gaze. "No, I'm fine."

She rolled her eyes but didn't say anything, just looked up at him with that sweet smile and sparkling eyes. And he felt himself relax. Actually relax, as if this was something he was comfortable doing, as if it was something he did every day.

The silence was companionable while they waited, comfortable and even welcoming. He didn't feel the need to make forced conversation, didn't feel the need to rack his brain for something, anything, to say.

Then they reached the window and it was their turn to order, and his mind went completely blank.

Not because he had no idea what to get. No, it was blank because it simply shut down when it registered what CC ordered.

He felt her eyes on him then finally looked down, wondering if his mouth was still open in surprise. Something must have shown on his face, because she laughed again, a sweet tinkling sound.

"Do not get between a woman and her chocolate, Big Guy. Now order something for yourself because I'm not sharing."

Dave looked up at the cashier, who was watching him expectantly, and realized he had no idea what he wanted. So he ordered a basic hot fudge sundae, then released her hand and reached into his back pocket for his wallet. He slid a sideways glance at CC, half-expecting her to argue about who would pay for it.

But she surprised him again with another soft laugh, shaking her head. "I'm not like a lot of other women, Big Guy. If someone is going to offer to buy me chocolate, the answer is always yes."

And for some reason, her answer didn't surprise him. For a day full of surprises, that was probably most surprising of all. So he pulled out some bills to pay for the ice cream then let CC lead him over to an empty table that was set slightly apart from the others. She took a seat, watching him as he lowered his large frame into the small metal chair.

Then he just sat there, not knowing what to say. He shifted, the chair squeaking with the movement, and wondered if it would break. At least that would give him something to talk about, he thought.

CC chuckled and he frowned at her in annoyance. Not because she was laughing at him, he knew she wasn't. But because laughter seemed to come so easy for her.

"I wish I had a camera so I could take a picture right now. You look so uncomfortable over there. Oh, wait. I do." She pulled her phone from her back pocket and, before Dave realized what she was about to do, she snapped a picture. She looked down at it, grinned, then turned the phone around and handed it to him.

With reluctance he accepted the phone, his fingers brushing against hers with a tingling awareness. He started, surprised, but she only grinned and released her hold on the phone.

The image on the screen showed a man in his early thirties, with deep set dark eyes, brows lowered in a partial scowl. A square jaw covered with a shadow of stubble. Small grooves bracketed lips pursed in annoyance.

No wonder CC kept calling him grumpy. The man in the picture looked perpetually pissed-off, and Dave wondered if that was how he looked all the time. The thought filled him with a weary sadness and a permeating sense of loss. Quickly on top of that came another emotion, fleeting but no less intense.

Anger.

Anger at the truth captured in that frozen second of time. Anger that he had allowed himself to become the man he glimpsed in the picture. His fingers tightened briefly against the phone, then relaxed as he handed it back to CC.

She was watching him carefully, her eyes studying, her oval face a blank mask hiding whatever she was thinking. Dave may have only just met her, but he knew that this sudden seriousness wasn't characteristic for her. He was sure she could be serious, had to be serious, given the nature of her job, but not like this.

He cleared his throat, looked away from her watchful gaze, turned back and tried to smile. It felt like a grimace. "I hope you're going to delete that."

CC suddenly smiled at him, all seriousness gone. Her thumb tapped at the phone's screen then she held it up for him to see. "All gone. Who knows, maybe one of these days, I'll get one of you smiling."

One of these days. She said it like she was sure there would be more days, more opportunities for candid pictures.

A chance she'd capture him smiling, for at least a frozen second in time.

Dave didn't know what to make of that, not when he wasn't even sure why he had called her tonight in the first place. And right now, he couldn't think past this minute, wouldn't consider anything past this hour, right here, right now.

But he couldn't tell her that and, thankfully, didn't have to, because the teenager bellowed their number from the window. Dave stood to pick up their order, then paused when he saw the tray being pushed their way.

One ice cream sundae, the clear plastic glass filled with two scoops of vanilla ice cream, drizzled in hot fudge, topped with whipped cream and a cherry.

And one monstrosity, dwarfing the sundae in size, drowning in so much hot fudge sauce, his back teeth hurt.

"Holy shit."

Laughter greeted his blunt observation as CC reached around him and grabbed the tray, along with some extra napkins. He turned and followed her back to their table, his eyes still rounded in amazement. She placed his sundae in front of him, then pulled the monstrosity in front of her, eyeing it with a broad grin.

"Are you actually going to eat that whole thing?" His words sounded almost accusing and he snapped his mouth shut, horrified that he had even asked something so rude. Because it was rude. Even ruder to ask that question of a woman he had invited out—not that this was a date or anything. Regardless, he would never say that to any woman he was out with, not if he had plans to ask her out again. CC deserved no less.

Even if this wasn't a date.

But instead of getting upset, or annoyed or impatient, she looked up at him with those clear laughing eyes and smiled. "Of course I am, Big Guy. I have to keep these curves somehow." She dipped the long plastic spoon into the monstrosity and scooped out a portion that was more fudge sauce than ice cream. His eyes followed the spoon's trail to her mouth, watched as her tongue darted out to lick the drip of fudge sauce hanging from the spoon. Her full lips closed over it and an expression of bliss crossed her face, her eyes closing in appreciation, a soft murmur accompanying the taste.

Dave was surprised his sundae didn't immediately melt from the instant heat that shot through him, just watching her. He closed his eyes and took a deep breath, opened them back up and glanced over at her.

"I think you have nice curves."

The words were out before he had even known they had formed in his mind, let alone traveled to his mouth. He snapped his mouth closed and looked down at the sundae in front of him, feeling his face heat. But CC only laughed, the sound light and musical. Teasing, but not in a mean way.

"Well I'll be. Did the Big Guy just give me a compliment? Or, horror, was he actually trying to flirt?"

Dave grumbled something and attacked his sundae, figuring his mouth couldn't get him into further trouble if it was shoved full of ice cream. CC laughed again and shook her head.

"And there it went. Oh well." She dipped her spoon into the fudge sauce and dug out another spoonful, bringing it to her mouth. Dave looked away, torn between responding to her comment, or drooling while watching her eat.

Either option would only lead him into more trouble. So he ate his sundae in silence, his gaze occasionally drifting across the table, watching. Not watching her eat, that was too much like torture, but just watching her.

And she did have nice curves. He'd have to be a blind monk not to appreciate them. Her body was fit and toned, he knew that from the brief time it had been pressed against him this morning. But she wasn't lean, wasn't stick thin, wasn't the kind of woman you'd be afraid to break if you held her too hard. She had curves. Nice, soft, full feminine curves, the kind that could cushion a man in all the right places if he was stretched out on top of her, driving deep—

He choked on a swallow of ice cream, so hard that tears welled in his eyes. Holy shit, where had that thought come from? He squeezed his eyes shut and coughed some more, trying to push the clear image from his mind. He had no business thinking like that, no business imagining how the woman across from him would look lying naked beneath him.

He choked again, his mind screaming *Liar*! He had been imagining just that since she had left his house this morning, he just didn't want to admit it.

"You okay over there?"

"Yeah." He coughed once more, cleared his throat. But he couldn't look at her, not when he was certain she would see every single thought reflected in his eyes. "Yeah. I'm fine."

She murmured something he couldn't make out and went back to her sundae. He looked down, surprised to see his was gone. And he searched his mind, looking for something to talk about, something safe and innocent to pass the time while she finished hers. His mind latched onto the one topic he figured was safe, grabbing at it with the desperation of a dying man.

"So how long have you been a Flight Medic?"

CC looked up at him through lowered lids, a smile lifting one corner of her mouth. She swallowed then chuckled. "Uh oh. Looks like we're treading in the safe harbor of small talk. And work is a safe topic, right?"

Dave opened his mouth to apologize, he wasn't

sure why, but she waved her hand between them, stopping him.

"No, it's all good." She took another bite of sundae, wiped her full mouth on a napkin, then sat back in her chair. "Eight years. I got my degree in Biological Sciences when I was twenty-one, along with my paramedic certification. I started applying around back home when I saw the notice for Flight Medic up here. I applied and got in, went through the academy, and thought I'd have to wait for a spot to open up. But they had open slots so I got moved over right after graduation. And here I am. How about you?"

"I've been in for twelve years, paramedic the entire time."

"Wow. The abbreviated version. I like it. Most times, guys won't shut up about themselves." She tilted her head, her long hair falling over one shoulder with the movement. "But somehow I get the impression that you don't open up much to anyone, so I'll stop myself from being too impressed."

Dave didn't say anything, once again not sure how to respond. It wasn't a feeling he was used to, and he was fairly certain he didn't like it. But CC didn't seem to notice. Or, if she did, she didn't say anything, just picked up the conversational ball and rolled with it.

"Let's see, what else would you like to know? I'm twenty-nine. Never been married. I'm originally from Georgetown, South Carolina. Middle child, only girl, Lord help me. Family is still all back home. I live by myself. No boyfriend, no pets, no kids." She paused, watching him, then smiled. "Okay, now it's your turn."

"My turn?"

"Yes, silly, that's how it works. I tell you about myself, then you tell me about yourself. Now it's your turn. Besides, my ice cream is melting."

He sat, stunned, as she went back to her sundae, her attention divided between what was left of the gooey monstrosity and him. But he didn't think for a minute that he could get away without answering, so he sat back in his own chair and let out a deep breath.

"Thirty-two. Lived in Maryland all my life. One sister. A father I haven't seen in almost ten years." Okay, he hadn't expected to tell her that. He reached down and grabbed the plastic spoon, rolling it back and forth in his hands. "Never been married. No girlfriend, no kids, no pets."

"See, already we have lots in common. Older or younger?"

"Pardon?"

"Your sister. Is she older or younger?"

"Younger. By almost eight years."

"Does she live with you? Or do you have that big house all to yourself?"

Dave clenched his jaw, surprised to feel irritation at the question. But if CC noticed, she didn't say anything, just looked at him with curiosity. He let out a heavy sigh and tossed the spoon back on the tray. "She moved out a few months ago, and I'm pretty sure she's going to be moving in with her boyfriend soon. He just bought a house."

"You don't sound happy about that."

Dave sighed and closed his eyes, thinking before he answered. Despite their recent estrangement, and all the reasons for it, he wanted to be happy for Angie. He *should* be happy for her. But he realized part of him was still pissed about how the entire thing had been handled, by all three of them. And for some reason, he didn't mind admitting it to the woman in front of him.

He opened his eyes to find her watching him, and gave her a small shrug. "Her boyfriend is a firefighter from my station that I've worked with for the last six years."

"Oh, I see." She nodded and finished the last bite of her sundae, then pushed the bowl to the middle of the table. And Dave realized she did see, that she understood without him trying to explain the tangle of illogical emotions that surrounded the entire situation.

Some of the tension left him, surprising him because he hadn't even realized he had been tense. He wasn't sure what to make of that.

"So what now, Big Guy?"

He looked up, not knowing how to read her question, not sure how to answer. And he realized that he seemed to be like that quite a bit around her: uncertain, never quite sure what was coming next. It was an unsettling realization, especially considering he had just met her.

Or maybe that was the reason behind the uncertainty.

"No idea, huh?" CC pushed back from the table and stood, then reached over and gathered their empties, placing everything neatly on the tray. "Well, I'm in the mood for a swim. You're more than welcome to join me."

He watched as she carried the tray to the counter, his eyes automatically dropping to her ass, hugged in faded denim. "I didn't bring a bathing suit."

CC turned back to him, one feathered brow lifted delicately as a smile spread across her face. "It's dark. Who needs a suit?"

A sudden desire that had nothing to do with swimming flooded through him, surprising him. Dave pushed back from the table and stood, one corner of his mouth tilting in a grimace that should have been a smile.

Because swimming suddenly sounded like the perfect way to end the night.

Chapter Five

CC dropped her keys on the coffee table and kept walking, Dave following her as she moved to the small hallway closet. He stopped and looked around, looking out of place and uncomfortable in all the color surrounding him.

"Nice place."

"So says the Big Guy with a scowl on his face." CC laughed as she pulled two fluffy beach towels from the closet, then wedged her hip against the door to close it all the way.

"No, it is. It's just..." His voice trailed off as he looked around him, and she knew exactly what he was going to say. Too bright, too colorful.

Too girlie.

He stood in the middle of the living room, surrounded by overstuffed furniture and bold splashes of blues and reds and greens. Bright, vibrant colors, full of life.

She threw one of the towels in his direction. "Not beige?"

His hands closed around the ball of material, fumbling a bit before folding it under one arm. He frowned, not missing her reference to the neutral décor that furnished his own house, then shook his head. "Definitely not beige, no."

She laughed and led the way out back, pausing on the porch to remove her boots and socks. She didn't look behind her, didn't pause or stop to think, just pulled her shirt over her head and tossed it on the wicker sofa then headed out the door and down the steps. The grass was damp under her bare feet, tickling her soles as she made her way to the pier. She heard Dave following behind her, heard him muttering under his breath. She couldn't catch the words, but the tone made her smile.

Confusion, bewilderment, disbelief. She had the impression he didn't do much spontaneously, and that he wasn't quite sure what to make of her.

Which suited her just fine.

She reached the pier and kept going, not stopping until she was at the end. She placed her towel on the bench then unsnapped her jeans and shimmied out of them. She folded them and placed them next to her towel, then stepped out of her underwear and tossed them on top. She turned, smiling when she saw Dave standing a few feet away, frozen as he watched her, hunger flashing in the depths of his eyes. She held his gaze as she reached behind her and unhooked her bra, letting the lacy material slide down her arms. His gaze dropped, settling on the fullness of her breasts.

She saw him swallow and she smiled again as she tossed the bra on top of her clothes. She straightened, letting him watch her for a few long seconds, then she turned and dove off the pier.

Cool water sluiced over her body, invigorating, refreshing. She glided under the water for a minute, then kicked to the surface and turned onto her back, treading water as she faced the pier.

Dave was standing at the end, uncertainty clear in every line of his body as he looked out over the water. He took a deep breath then peeled off his shirt, moonlight caressing his broad chest. CC watched, waiting, her breath held as his fingers worked the zipper of his jeans. He pushed them down to his hips then paused, his eyes finding hers.

"How deep is it?" His voice was deep, gruff. Uncertain.

She swallowed a groan, the anticipation almost killing her. Didn't he realize how much she wanted to see him? All of him, that magnificent body bared to just the moon—and her eyes. Was he deliberately teasing her, or was he really that obtuse?

She lowered her face into the water and exhaled through her mouth, bubbles of frustration breaking the smooth dark surface. He must be obtuse. She didn't think he had a teasing bone in his body.

She swam a little closer to the pier and looked up at him. "Deep enough. You're not going to break your neck diving in, if that's what you're worried about."

He frowned and she held her breath, waiting. And finally, finally, he pushed the jeans down and off. And he had been going commando all night, because there he was, bared to her hungry eyes in his full glory.

She sunk a little lower in the water, hiding her smile of appreciation at what she saw. Dear sweet Jesus, there was a little slice of heaven right there, bared in all its glory for her eyes only.

And yeah, *little* it wasn't.

He caught her looking at him and another frown crossed his face before he dove in, splitting the water in a smooth arc as he disappeared beneath the surface.

But not before she had seen his impressive anatomy harden, lengthen under her gaze. She smiled then swam away from the pier, guessing, judging before she stopped.

And smiled even more when Dave surfaced less than a foot away with a gasp of surprise.

"Holy shit, why didn't you tell me how cold it was?"

"Not too cold, I hope." She gave him a meaningful smile, laughing at the embarrassment on his face as he caught her meaning. She smacked her hand against the surface, splashing him, then kicked off and swam away.

Her strokes were long and powerful, her muscles stretching, warming, with each movement. Water caressed her skin, cool against her flesh, but doing nothing to calm the fire burning inside, simmering beneath the surface of her skin.

She dove, kicking down, down until her hand sunk into the soft mud at the bottom. She flipped then turned, closing her legs in one powerful kick before shooting to the surface. Water dripped from her hair, running into her face, and she tossed her head, flipping the wet hair out of her eyes, then turned back toward the pier. Dave was treading water, watching her, his eyes following her every move until she stopped next to him.

"You know, the whole purpose of swimming is to actually move around and swim."

"Hm?" He blinked and shook his head, as if just remembering where he was and what he was doing. She moved a little closer, close enough that she could feel the heat of his body through the water separating him. His eyes caught hers, burning, intense. The urge to tease him vanished, replaced with a different urge, stronger, more primal.

She reached her hand toward him, her fingers brushing against the hardness of his broad chest. His breath hissed between them, his body tightening beneath her touch. Time slowed, the air around them becoming heavy, thick.

One of his arms came around her, pulling her through the water until their bodies pressed together. She wrapped her legs around his waist, the rigid length of his erection hard against her bottom. All she had to do was tilt her hips, thrust toward him and—

His mouth crashed down on hers, hungry, feeding. She groaned as his tongue swept against hers, a frenzy of need exploding with each touch. Her body melted against his, heat exploding between them.

She wanted, needed. All of him.

She broke away with a groan of desperation then kicked off, shooting through the water until she reached the pier. Her hand closed around the ladder and she turned, facing him with a smile.

"As much as I want this, I don't want to drown doing it. Come here."

But he didn't move and for a long minute she mentally swore at herself, wondering if she had just ruined everything. If, by moving away too soon, she had given him time to think about what they were doing.

Time to change his mind.

But then he was next to her, moving so quickly she didn't see him, just felt the warmth of his large, hard body next to hers. His mouth was on hers again, his hands gliding over her breasts, her waist, her thighs. His touch was hungry, desperate, feeding on her own hunger. She wrapped her legs around him, her hips searching until the tip of his cock was pressed against her, throbbing, ready.

He pulled his mouth from hers, a scowl on his face. "I don't have any condoms—"

"I'm on birth control." She tilted her hips, rubbing against him, wondering what he would say, what he would do. His jaw clenched and his head tilted back, but only for a second before he looked at her again.

"That's not the only thing to worry about."

"I'm tested regularly. Part of the job. Not that I've ever had to worry." She rolled her hips against once more, waiting. "You?"

He groaned, shook his head. "Clean. No worries."

The words hung between them, expectant, cautious, begging for a trust that hadn't yet been earned. CC still didn't know what had gotten into her, why she was so willing to cross lines that she had never crossed before. Why she was so willing to trust the man in front of her. She only knew it was right.

And it was what she wanted. Reckless, dangerous, and all too tempting.

Dave's eyes captured hers, dark, intense, studying her too closely. But she didn't look away, could hardly breathe as he watched her. Then he groaned, the sound deep and strangled, before his mouth crashed against hers once more. Was he feeling just as reckless, just as dangerous as she? Or was she only imagining his hunger, projecting her own onto him?

He deepened the kiss, his body moving closer against hers, his hands drifting along her legs, kneading, caressing. Down her thighs, to her knees, bending and spreading her legs as his cock teased her.

Down further to her calves.

And then he froze, his eyes snapping open and impaling her with an expression she couldn't read. She swallowed and reached above her, her hands closing around each side of the ladder, supporting her as his right hand gently caressed her calf, feeling, searching. Learning.

"What happened?" His voice was rough, hoarse, hollow in the echo of the night and water around them. She saw curiosity in his gaze, curiosity and concern.

But not revulsion, not judgment.

Her heart squeezed, beat hard for a few seconds, then melted, sending a different kind of warmth through her. She smiled and tilted her hips against him.

"Do you really want to talk about this now?"

"No. God, no." He growled and slid his hands to her hips, his fingers digging into her flesh as he drove into her in one sudden thrust, spreading her, filling her.

Her head dropped back as sound escaped her, part scream, part moan, loud and long. Her legs spread wider as she took all of him in, deep, hard. He held himself still, his mouth nipping at the flesh between her neck and shoulder as a shudder went through him.

"Jesus, you're so fucking tight. Tight and wet."

She smiled then bit down on her lower lip as he pulled out, pushed back in. Slow, agonizingly slow, teasing. She wanted more, all of it. Hard, fast, deep.

But his hands tightened against her hips, his grip on her a vice, holding her still as he moved against her, inside her, slow, so slow.

His teeth nipped her flesh again, then moved up her neck, nibbling her ear, tasting, teasing, as he pulled out, then entered her again. Slow, pushing against her, his hips grinding into hers.

Her head drifted back, resting against the step of the ladder as her hands held tight above her. Liquid fire, hot, searing, shot out from her center, down along her limbs, melting her inside and out. And still Dave moved slowly, each thrust, each withdrawal smooth, deliberate, teasing.

Driving her insane, driving her to the brink of surrender. And she realized that, in this, she had no control. By backing herself against the ladder for support, she had inadvertently given him all control.

In this, at least, she was willing to surrender.

His lips closed over hers, swallowing her small cries as his tongue thrust into her, tasting, claiming as his hips mimicked the motion. Stronger, harder, just a little faster.

Her legs tightened around him, holding him closer, her heels digging into the tight muscles of his ass. He thrust into her, filling her, pulled back, then thrust again. Her muscles quivered, tightened around him, desperate to hold him inside her.

He pulled his mouth from hers, his eyes searching out her gaze, desire flaming in their dark depths. She bit down on her lower lip as he pushed into her, pushing her closer to the edge then pulling her back, refusing to let her fly.

"What's my name?"

She smiled, damning him at the same time she answered on a breathy sigh. "Big Guy."

He thrust into her, pulled away, shook his head. "What's my name?"

Damn him, she was so close. She moaned, closed her eyes. "Oh God."

"Not quite." He thrust once more, harder, deeper

as he laughed against her mouth. The sound was musical, magical, filling her with surprise.

And something else, something she couldn't define. She shattered, exploding around him, shards of light piercing her eyes. Her hands dropped to his shoulders, her fingers digging into his flesh as her head fell back. The muscles in her legs, her back, her entire body tightened as she convulsed around him, squeezing, gripping. His name tore from her lips on a soft scream.

"Dave."

His mouth crashed down on hers, swallowing her cries as his rhythm increased. Harder, faster, deeper. Water splashed around them, cooling her skin from the outside as Dave's heat burned her inside.

His hands left her hips, wrapped around the ladder behind her ass as he pounded into her. Over and over, harder, faster.

She exploded again, cresting, crashing. He ripped his mouth from hers, his head flung back, his strong jaw clenched.

Thrust. Deep, in, out. Once more.

His hips ground into hers as a long growl tore from his chest, the sound rumbling around them, touching something inside her as he exploded inside her, filling her.

Seconds went by, silently stretching into minutes. Their ragged breaths mingled, echoing around them, becoming one, slowing as waves turned into gentle ripples that lapped at their joined bodies.

CC closed her eyes, breathing hard, her hands slowly relaxing against his shoulders. She felt his mouth close over hers in a soft, lingering kiss, felt his forehead drop and rest against her shoulder. His arms shook around her but his grip remained strong on the ladder, anchoring them in place as their bodies floated, weightless, in the water.

"Jesus." Dave's voice was barely a whisper, his breath hot against her neck as another shudder ran through him. Or maybe her, she couldn't tell. She smiled, turned her head and dropped a kiss on his temple, sighing.

Minutes continued to stretch around them, neither of them moving, content to remain suspended in each other's arms. Another shiver went through her, this one from the chill of the water against their skin. Dave shifted and she moaned at his loss, felt his lips press against her neck before he moved away.

She opened her eyes, her heart skipping when she saw him smiling at her, his eyes crinkling ever so slightly at the corners. The breath hitched in her chest at the sight and she reached out, the tips of her fingers tracing the lines of his mouth.

"You have a beautiful smile."

He smiled again, briefly, before he kissed the tips of her fingers. Their eyes met and held, a thousand wordless thoughts passing between them in the space of a heartbeat. She smiled, lowered her hand, reached around and squeezed his tight ass. Then she turned and grabbed the ladder, climbing up on shaking legs. She grabbed her towel and handed the other to Dave as he reached the pier and stood next to her.

Water dripped from his body, all hard planes and muscle. She swallowed, content to watch as he rubbed the towel across his body. Then she smiled and turned away, heading back to the house. "I'm starving. Do you want something to eat?"

His laughter, low and melting, filled her with

warmth as he followed her into the house.

Chapter Six

The early light of dawn drifted into the room, filtered through the curtains billowing in the cool breeze. He should still be asleep, he thought. Burrowed under the covers, his skin chilled.

He was anything but.

He shifted, stretching out along the bed, the heat of CC's body warming him. She was on her stomach, lying perpendicular to him, her legs stretched across his lap, her head and arms almost hanging off the other side of the bed. He ran his hand up her leg, smiling at her soft moan as he rubbed her ass. Then he ran his hand back down, his fingers kneading the heavy muscle of her thigh, tickling the sensitive spot behind her knee, further down to the mangled spot that used to be a shapely calf.

Both hands cradled her leg, rubbing at the torn flesh and rough scar tissue, alternating between hard pressure and gentle caress. He leaned down and pressed his lips against the deep hollow where flesh had been sewn over missing muscle, heard her sigh

71

softly at the touch.

"Most guys freak out when they see it." Her voice was a whisper, nearly lost against the thick comforter. A spurt of anger, unexpected and surprising, surged through him.

"I'm not most guys."

"No." She shifted, looking over her shoulder at him, a soft smile on her peaceful face. "No, you're not."

He grunted, making her chuckle before she rested her head against the edge of the mattress and closed her eyes. His hands continued stroking her leg in gentle circles.

"When did it happen?"

"About three years ago, just outside Bagram."

"IED?"

She made a sound that wasn't quite a laugh and shook her head, giving him a half-smile. "Not every mangled limb is from an IED, you know."

"Yeah, I do know."

Her eyes softened, became serious as she watched him. She reached back with her hand and squeezed his arm. "Yeah, I guess you do."

He looked away, knowing she was seeing too much, much more than he wanted her to see. For now. For now? He gave himself a mental shake. No, not just for now—forever.

Dave shifted again, resumed massaging her leg, and let out a deep breath. "So, not an IED."

"Bullet fire. We were moving equipment when we were ambushed. Everyone dove for cover. You'd think for as small as I am, I wouldn't have trouble finding a hiding place." She laughed, but the sound was forced, almost bitter.

"So you took bullet fire into your leg."

"Yeah, well. It was better than letting them tear into the soldier I was taking care of."

Jesus. He closed his eyes, the scene vivid in his mind, only because he had lived it too often in real life. Patching up wounds, praying for the best, wishing you could do more. The sudden burst of machine gun fire, the whine of bullets spraying, the dull thud and screams when they found their target.

Throwing yourself over the patient, protecting them with your own body, doing what you had to do to get them out alive. Or at least get them out so they had a chance.

His hands stilled for a minute, then resumed their slow massage.

"So what was your MOS? Health Care Specialist?" He wasn't sure why he asked, fairly certain that she was going to answer yes. It would fit, given her training. But that didn't mean she would have been safer, because women were only marginally safer in the desert. No, they still didn't serve in the infantry back then, weren't in the middle of the battle.

But that only worked when the battleground was clearly drawn, something that hadn't been clear for too many years now.

He heard her laugh, looked up in surprise to see a small smile tilt one corner of her mouth before she answered. "Not quite. 94 Echo."

Dave paused, thinking he hadn't heard her correctly. His brows pulled down in a frown and he stared at her. "You did radio and communications repair?"

"Yup. Not what you were expecting, was it?"

"What the hell were you doing over there repairing electronics, especially with your qualifications?"

"Because I wanted to broaden my horizons when I joined the Reserves, learn something new just in case I wanted a career change down the line."

"And yet you still nearly got killed saving someone."

"Yeah, well, old habits kicked in." She closed her eyes and turned her head away, but not before he saw the flash of pain cross her face. He sighed and tightened his hands around her calf, then moved her legs and shifted so he was lying beside her. He wrapped his arms around her waist and pulled her close, pressing a kiss to the top of her head.

"He didn't make it, did he?" It was a statement more than a question, his voice quiet because he already knew the answer. She breathed in deeply, let her breath out slowly, and shook her head, the movement barely perceptible. His arms tightened around her and he just held her, knowing there was nothing else he could say or do.

They stayed that way for long minutes, their bodies warm despite the cool gentle breeze coming through the open windows. Dave closed his eyes, not thinking, not worrying, just feeling.

At ease. Content in just this moment.

CC turned in his arms so she was facing him, her head tucked against his shoulder, her hand tracing lazy circles around his chest, down to his stomach, back up again. He had been half-hard for the last hour, despite their topic of conversation. Her touch rectified that instantly, and he felt her smile against his chest. Her fingers skimmed along his breastbone, their touch feather light as they moved lower, lower until she traced his length with one short, neatly manicured nail.

He sucked his breath in with a sharp hiss when her

hand closed around him, her grip sure, her strokes long and steady. She pushed up on her elbow, the ends of her long hair teasing his chest, then leaned over. Over, down, until her mouth closed over him.

His hands fisted in the comforter beneath him, his hips thrusting up, urging her to take more of him. The wet heat of her mouth surrounded him, sucking, nipping. He moaned her name then could think of nothing else, his mind suddenly blank, empty of everything except mindless pleasure, mindless need.

And CC wouldn't stop, her hands stroking his legs, cupping his balls as she sucked, teased, licked. Dave moaned and thrust his hips up, once, twice. He reached down and threaded his fingers in her hair, the silky strands wrapping around his hands. He was torn between holding her in place and thrusting deeper, harder into her mouth.

Or pulling her up and thrusting deep into another tight, inviting, warmth.

She wrested the decision away from him, wrapping her arms around his thighs, holding him in place.

Imprisoning him.

Her mouth worked its magic, hot, slick, as she sucked. Her tongue swirled around the head of his swollen cock before she lowered herself on him, taking all of him, the suction of her mouth squeezing, urging.

He thrust his hips once more, his hands tightening against her head as he exploded, filling her mouth. He lay back on the bed, his chest heaving, expecting her to pull away.

But she didn't stop, just swallowed and kept sucking, her mouth gentling, her touch easing until he thought he'd go insane from the sensation. She moaned, a soft breath against his thigh, then kissed her way back up his body. He tightened his arms around her waist and pulled her flush against him, then ran his hands along her back, up through her hair.

He pulled her mouth down against his, kissing her deeply, thoroughly, before pulling away with a sigh. His eyes drifted to her hair, watching the play of light through the silky strands, turning it into shades of gold and honey.

"Your hair is so beautiful."

She smiled and leaned forward, dropping a kiss on his chin before resting her head on his chest. His arms came around her once more, his hand drawing lazy circles on her back.

And he realized that not once since he had met CC for ice cream last night had stress or worry over anything bothered him. Not once had thoughts of anonymous text messages or threats crossed his mind.

And he realized he could stay here for hours, just like this, with nothing more important than holding CC in his arms. God, how he wished he could. For right now, for this moment in time, he wanted nothing more.

CC pushed up from her spot against his chest, her hazel eyes meeting his. "Hm. Why do I think I'm losing you already?"

He leaned up and pressed a kiss against her lips. "No. Not losing."

"Maybe." She softened the doubt that laced her simple word with a smile, her gaze still steady on his. Then she sighed and rolled off him, her momentum taking her to the edge of the bed until she lowered her legs off the side and stood up. The action was so smoothly done, so quick and efficient that Dave smiled again.

He rolled to his side, watching as she rounded the bed and walked toward the bathroom, her shapely ass bared to his gaze, bathed in early morning light. She glanced over her shoulder and grinned, then closed the door.

Disappointment surged through him at the loss of view.

At the loss of her.

He rolled to his back and scrubbed his hands over his face, staring up at the ceiling fan. The blades turned in a slow hypnotic circle, their lazy rotation lulling him into a trance.

The sound of running water came through the closed door and Dave tilted his head, listening. It sounded like the sink, not the shower.

Which was a shame, because he wouldn't have minded joining CC in the shower. Yeah, he would have definitely volunteered to scrub her back for her.

What the hell was he doing? He shook his head and called himself every kind of fool. He didn't need to be lounging in her bed, thinking of ways to convince her to come back in and join him. He was certain she had things to do, just like he did.

Like getting a new cell phone to replace the one he had shattered yesterday.

Cold fingers of reality danced across his skin, chilling him. He cursed then pushed himself off the bed, walking toward the overstuffed chair where he had thrown his clothes when they had come inside last night.

He tugged on his jeans, wincing as he adjusted himself before pulling on the zipper. Christ, how could he still be semi-hard, after last night? After this morning? He shook his head and yanked on his shirt, then sat down on the chair and shook out his socks before putting them on.

Where were his shoes? He looked around, wondering what he had done with them, then looked up when the bathroom door opened.

CC leaned against the doorway, watching him with a small smile on her face. She was wearing a baggy pair of sweatpants and a loose t-shirt.

And no bra. Dave swallowed, trying not to notice the full breasts that pushed against the loose material. His face heated and he looked away, clearing his throat.

CC laughed and walked over to him, resting a hand on each side of the chair before leaning down and kissing him. She pulled away too soon and straightened. "Your shoes are on the back porch. I'll go get them for you."

Dave followed her out of the room and out to the back porch, part of his mind still wondering what excuse he could use to stay. Just for a little longer—

CC stopped so suddenly, he nearly slammed into her back and had to put his hand against the screen door to stop himself. Her body stilled, becoming tense and alert in the space of heart beat. She turned and put her hand in middle of his chest, pushing him back into the house with such force he stumbled.

"What the—"

"Get back, now." She pushed again, still not looking at him. Her attention was riveted at a spot near the exterior porch door, her own alertness seeping into him. Adrenaline pumped through his veins as he tried to peer over her shoulder, wondering what in the hell had caused the sudden change in her.

She took a step back and collided against his chest.

Dave's arms came up instinctively to grab her shoulders but she shrugged them off and turned toward him. A frown creased her forehead as she looked up at him, her clear eyes cold and remote.

"Is there something you maybe want to tell me, Big Guy?

Icy dread blew through Dave's stomach but he wasn't sure why. He started to shake his head, stopped, then leaned past CC to see what had caused her sudden change.

A fist knotted his gut, twisting with razor-sharp dread.

Wedged against the door, propped against his shoes, was a small poster board-size sheet of paper, splattered in what looked like blood. And scrawled across the page, in bold letters, were the words he had become too familiar with over the last eight months.

I know what you did.

Chapter Seven

Stillness had descended over the colorful room, muting the bright colors with an air of tension, of expectation. Of anxiety and accusation. Dave sat on the edge of the overstuffed chair, absurdly feeling like he was being sucked into it.

Like he had been sucked into this nightmare so many months ago.

He looked down at the clasped hands hanging between his legs, the knuckles pale and tight. He took a deep breath and held it, then released it slowly as he tried to relax his hands.

"Here. It looks like you could use this."

CC held out a glass tumbler filled with dark amber liquid. He reached up to take it from her, somewhat surprised to see the slight shaking of his hand. If she saw it, she didn't say anything, just gave him the glass and took a seat in the matching chair next to his.

Dave lifted the glass to his mouth and took a long swallow, grimacing as the heat of the strong brandy seared his throat and hit his stomach with a fiery punch. He wasn't usually a brandy drinker but he wasn't about to turn down a shot of anything strong.

The police had left about thirty minutes ago, after doing a cursory search around the place and asking him questions. They took notes, asked more questions, looked around some more. One of the officers—there had been five of them, which had surprised him at first—had called Dave's friend to verify that he had reported similar incidents in the past.

Yes, he had reported them.

No, not all of them.

The last incident? Dave couldn't help the short laugh that had escaped him when he answered. Yesterday morning.

Through it all, CC had remained quiet, leaning against the wall, her arms folded in front of her as she watched him. She had changed into jeans and a t-shirt.

And a huge fucking .45 Glock strapped to her hip that looked like it would knock her on her ass if she fired it. But not before it put a hole the size of a cannon into whatever fool made the mistake of crossing her.

Because she was a cop. Something Dave had forgotten. Yes, she was a Flight Medic. But she was, first and foremost, a cop.

He took another swallow of the brandy then swirled the glass in his hands, staring down into the dark liquid, watching as it briefly clung to the sides of the glass before drifting down.

He knew he needed to leave, needed to go home and do—well, he wasn't entirely certain what he needed to do, but he knew there was something.

Go buy a new phone.

And a pair of new shoes while he was it, since his other ones had been taken as evidence. Evidence of what, he didn't know, since the officers had told him they didn't think they'd find out who was behind this.

But they'd try, and get back to him.

And they *would* try. Because CC was one of them, and this had happened here, at her house.

Because of him.

"Shit." He raised the glass, thought better of it, then leaned forward and sat it on the coffee table. He ran his hands through his hair then glanced at CC. She was still sitting in the chair, her legs curled beneath her, watching him. "I'm sorry."

Her brows arched, either in surprise or in question, Dave didn't know. She took a sip of her own drink, her gaze never leaving his. "You're sorry for...?"

He wanted to look away from those clear bright eyes, afraid she'd see too much. But he didn't, he couldn't. "For all of it. For allowing this to happen here. For bringing you into it. For embarrassing you in front of your friends. For making them wonder what I was even doing here, so early in the morning."

CC watched him for a second, took another sip, then leaned forward and placed her glass next to his. When she looked back up at him, one corner of her mouth was tilted in a hint of a smile. "Wow, that's a lot to be sorry about."

"Well, I am."

"Hm. Why don't we start with point one? First, you didn't 'allow' this. That implies that you knew some whack doodle was going to show up here while you knowingly looked the other way while he did what he did. Second, you didn't bring me into this, the whack doodle did." He opened his mouth to interrupt, but she held her hand up in warning and leaned closer. "Third and fourth, what in the world do I have to be embarrassed about, and why would I care what any of them might think about you being here?"

"I—" Dave snapped his mouth closed, not knowing what to say. Any other person would be upset, or angry, or even a little fearful, if not outright scared. And they'd have every right to be. Hell, even he was worried about what was going on, because of the unknown of the entire situation. He couldn't believe that the woman sitting next to him was taking this whole thing in stride. "I can't believe none of this upsets you."

"I never said I wasn't upset." She briefly pursed her lips, then leaned over and placed a hand on his arm. "But I'm not upset with *you*." She squeezed his arm then leaned over and grabbed his drink, handing it to him before she took hers.

He wanted to ask her what upset her, because to his eyes, at least, she didn't look the least bit upset. But she must have read his mind because she shifted in the chair and tilted her head, watching him.

"I know. I don't look upset. Trust me, I am. Some psycho was creeping around my house in the middle of the night, and I didn't even know it. That bothers me."

"I'm sorry. This is my fault. I should have never even come here."

"Let me ask you a question. Has your stalker ever followed you anywhere before? Left you notes like this anywhere else?"

A chill danced along his spine when he heard the word 'stalker'. And as much as he didn't want to admit it, he knew it was true. Something had changed, making this escalate from harassment to something much more sinister.

And he felt completely, utterly helpless and

unprepared to deal with it.

CC was watching him and he realized he still hadn't answered her question. He shook his head. "No, never. Nothing like this. I told you, it's just been the text messages, all saying essentially the same thing."

"That you know of." It was a statement, not a question, and the implication sent icy shards through him.

"Yeah. That I know of. And now he knows where you live." Dave put his glass on the table then pushed himself out of the chair, the brandy forming a sour pool of acid in his gut. "I need to leave. I'm sorry."

CC's hand snaked out and closed around his wrist, stopping him. She stood up, standing closer to him, her hand sliding down until her fingers threaded through his. Her eyes were soft, understanding.

And he couldn't understand why.

"Where are you going?"

"Home, which is where I should have stayed last night."

"I see." Her fingers squeezed his then let go, but she didn't move away, just kept looking up at him. "And is that number five?"

"Five?" Dave shook his head, not understanding.

"Yeah. The fifth thing you're sorry about. Coming here last night."

How was he supposed to answer that? Hell no, he wasn't sorry about their time spent together. But he was sorry as hell that he had brought this mess, literally, to her door. Would he do it all over again, knowing what he knew now? The answer should be no, he wouldn't. But he didn't know if he could say that and still be honest. Not with memories of last night, of this morning, so clear in his mind.

"CC, if I hadn't come here last night, you wouldn't have been involved. So yeah, I wish I would have just stayed home."

"I see. But, are you sorry about what happened?"

"Between us? No. No, I'm not sorry about that."

"Good. Neither am I." Her lips widened in a smile as she fisted her hand in his shirt and pulled him down, closer, until her lips pressed against his. He held himself still for the space of a heartbeat, certain they were both crazy, then wrapped his arms around her and pulled her even closer.

The kiss was too short, yet he was still breathing heavy when she pulled away.

"Well, then. Let's get you home." She smiled up at him again then started walking away, leaving Dave staring after her in confusion. She was almost out of the room when he finally found his voice.

"What do you mean, 'us'?"

She looked over her shoulder, her long hair swinging against her back. "Just what I said. I'm the one with the gun, remember?"

"Yeah. I do now. But that doesn't mean—"

"You don't have a choice in the matter, Big Guy, okay?"

"But—"

"No buts. Gun, remember?"

He gritted his teeth, knowing he was losing the argument and not sure why. Hell, he wasn't even sure what the argument was. His mind whirled, searching for something, anything, to sway her from following him home. He didn't need her there, didn't want to drag her into his own personal mess any more than he already had. In desperation, he blurted out the first thing that came to mind, something completely senseless and inane.

"About that gun. If you were a guy, I'd ask what you were over-compensating for."

Whatever reaction he hoped for, it wasn't her sudden laughter. He gritted his teeth again, knowing he had already lost the battle. Probably before it even started.

"You've already seen everything I have, Big Guy. I guess you can answer better than I if I'm compensating for anything. As for the gun, don't worry. I just like how it freaks people out when they see it. It amuses me."

She winked then walked out of the room, leaving him staring after her, his jaw still clenched and his face heating in embarrassment.

It amused her to freak people out. Dave knew he should be surprised, but he wasn't. He had only just met her, but already learned that she thrived on the unexpected.

And yeah, on top of everything else that had happened in the last thirty-six hours, it freaked him out a bit to realize he already knew that about her.

Chapter Eight

The air in the hangar was cool. The scent of early autumn mixed with the saltier brackish smell of the nearby water, adding a slight tang to the air. CC breathed in deeply, inhaling the crisp air as her boot steps echoed against the concrete floor. She loved this time of year, the crisp air and rich colorful scents. Her dad's voice rang in the back of her mind, calling her nuts, telling her you couldn't see smells, and she almost smiled.

Almost.

But she had too much on her mind right now to spare time thinking about home and her parents. She missed them, missed her brothers, and knew she was overdue for a visit.

But she didn't have time to spare for that right now, either.

She climbed into the passenger compartment of the helicopter, scooting in on her butt, then began her daily inspection. The routine was soothing, familiar, almost as natural as breathing. Equipment checks, inventory, the act of checking to make sure everything was where it should be.

Just as she liked it.

She ran down the list, checking each item off, both on paper and in her mind. One last look around, just to be sure she didn't miss anything, then she scrawled her signature at the bottom of the sheet and climbed down.

She'd file this, then catch up on her other reports. That was the one thing she hated the most: paperwork. No matter how much time she spent on it, there always seemed to be more waiting. Probably because that was the one thing she couldn't seem to do quickly, no matter how much time she allowed herself.

Of course, even she admitted that it wouldn't take quite so long to do if she actually filled out the paperwork, instead of staring at the reports and letting her mind wander aimlessly until she lost all track of time. At least she was honest enough with herself to admit that she wasn't a paperwork kind of person. Never had been, probably never would be.

She pushed through the swinging doors that connected the hangar to the office and living quarters, then turned into the radio room and tossed the clipboard on the desk. She crossed the hall into the small area that passed for a breakroom and made a beeline for the coffee pot.

Tony Fordham, her partner and pilot, looked up from the newspaper and watched her. "Heard you had some excitement at your place the other night."

"Of course you did. Heaven forbid anything remain a secret around this place. And they say women gossip." She offered him a smile as she took a sip of the strong coffee then sat at the table across from him.

"So what was the story by the time you heard it? Mutilated bodies? Sex orgies? Murder and mayhem?"

Tony laughed, folding the paper neatly in half before tossing it to the middle of the table. "Nah. Just heard that some psycho left a threatening note on your porch, but that it was meant for your 'friend'."

"Wow, not bad. I figured it would have been exaggerated into something more exciting by now." CC reached for the paper, pointedly ignoring Tony's questioning look. Less than a minute went by before he pulled the paper away and fixed her with a steady gaze from his cool green eyes.

"So you want to share the details?"

"Not particularly, no."

Tony tugged harder on the paper, finally pulling it away from her. "That's not going to fly with me and you know it. Spill it. Who's the guy?"

CC rolled her eyes then took another sip of coffee. "He's a paramedic with the county."

"And?"

"And what? And nothing."

"Really?" He leaned back in the chair and folded his arms across his chest. "And he just happened to come visiting at seven in the morning, hm?"

"What can I say? He's an early riser." CC mentally flinched at her choice of words, a vivid image clearly forming in her mind of just how much of an early riser Big Guy really was.

"Holy shit, you're blushing!"

"I am not, now hush."

"Yes, you are. Your cheeks are all pink and blotchy. That's definitely a blush."

"No, it's not. It's irritation from you bugging me."

"Hmm-mm. So, does this guy have a name?

Where'd you meet him? How long have you known him?"

"What is this, the third degree? You're worse than my brother."

"I'm your surrogate brother, so start talking."

CC turned in her seat and grabbed for the paper, deliberately ignoring him. She knew it wouldn't work, but there was no way she was going to answer Tony's questions.

Especially not the one about how long she'd known Dave. No way. Because the answer just sounded all wrong and she'd never hear the end of it.

"Fine. I'll drop it for now. Tell me about this threatening note."

CC dropped the paper to the table with a sigh, knowing she'd get no chance to read it until answering at least a few of Tony's questions. She shook her head. Not in refusal to answer, but rather in hesitation, trying to figure out how to explain.

On the surface, the note and texts were disturbing, which was bad enough. But underneath, there was something more sinister, something that sent a chill racing along her spine. But she couldn't pinpoint it, couldn't even begin to explain it. It was just something she *felt*.

"It really wasn't that bad." CC felt some irrational need to downplay it. "It was just a handwritten note on a piece of poster board. *I know what you did.* Whoever left it splashed paint on it, making it look like blood."

Tony's expression hardened, his blue eyes going cold as the muscle in his jaw ticked. He watched her in silence then shook his head, anger clear on his weathered face. "And this note was left on your back porch? In the middle of the night? While you were home?"

Okay, so maybe it sounded as bad as it was. But she wasn't about to admit to Tony how much seeing it had rattled her. Yes, she could admit to herself it had freaked her out a bit. More than a bit. Someone had been next to her house, actually on her screened-in porch. And she hadn't even known. That freaked her out almost more than the note itself.

"I think maybe you should stay away from this guy. Sounds like he's deep into something you want no parts of."

"Not happening." CC shook her head, just in case Tony didn't understand the words. Her partner could be stubborn when he wanted to be. "I like him. Besides, I'm kind of already involved, since it was my house and all."

"Then get uninvolved. What kind of guy would willingly drag a woman into his trouble? Not one you want to be with, I'll tell you that much."

"Tony, it's not like that. From what he said, he's been getting text messages for eight months, and this is the first time anything like this has happened."

"Yeah, from what he said. You don't know what he hasn't been telling you. For all you know, this guy could be doing it himself. Or something."

"He's not."

"And how do you know that? Wait, let me guess, you just do."

"Knock it off. And don't make fun of me and my feelings. Sometimes I do just know."

"One of these days, you're going to be wrong. And then what?"

"Then I use my .45 and won't have to worry about it."

"You know, sometimes I think you just have a death wish. You're not happy unless your courting trouble or danger or whatever the hell it is that gets your blood pumping."

CC narrowed her eyes at him, letting him know that they were not having this conversation. Again. Yes, she liked adventure. No, she didn't have a death wish. She had been there, done that, had no desire to go there again, thank you very much.

Tony narrowed his own eyes at her, starting one of their occasional staring matches, two strong-willed people not daring to give an inch. Fortunately, her phone rang, giving her an excuse to look away.

"'Lo?"

"It's Rob. I've got that information you asked for."

"Bubby! Wow, that was fast."

Her brother's heavy sigh came through the phone and she could clearly imagine him rolling his eyes. Or reaching up to pinch the bridge of his nose. Or both.

"Stop calling me that. I'm not twelve anymore. And neither are you." He paused. "Carolann."

CC scowled into the phone then pushed away from the table. She didn't want to have this conversation in front of Tony. And she didn't want to get into a game of one-upmanship with her older brother so she ignored his use of her full name, spoken with an exaggerated drawl.

"Tell me what you got." CC walked out of the hangar and squinted in the bright sun, then pulled her sunglasses down to shield her eyes.

"Tell me again who this guy is to you."

CC rolled her eyes. "A friend."

Silence greeted her answer and CC did her best not to huff in impatience. If Bubby's heavy sigh was any indication, she hadn't been very successful.

"Hm. Well, your friend is squeaky clean. Nothing in here that you wouldn't have been able to find out yourself. Exemplary service record, a couple of commendations. Honorable discharge from the Reserves, came out as an E6. Nothing out of the ordinary." She heard the sound of his fingers clicking against a keyboard in the background. "You going to tell me again why you wanted me to check?"

"Just curious, that's all."

"Wouldn't have anything to do with those police reports that popped up when I checked, would it?"

CC grimaced, glad her brother couldn't see her face. Damn him. But she should have known he'd look deeper when she asked him to check on Dave's record. Not his public record. Bubby was right, she could access that if she wanted to do. No, she was curious about any not-so-public record, something that might explain why he was receiving these threats.

And Bubby could access things that didn't exist.

"I have no idea what you're talking about."

"You know I can tell when you're lying, right?" He paused, and CC knew that he was definitely pinching the bridge of his nose in exasperation. But she didn't say anything, unwilling to admit anything. "Of course, you already know about that. So what are you looking for?"

"A connection."

"This one of your hunches?"

"No, more than a hunch." Like insider information, coming straight from the Big Guy himself when he told her more about some of the text messages he received. "Anything in there on his time in Helmand Province?"

"Nothing out of the ordinary. He was in the middle of it, no doubt. As a medic, I'm sure he saw a lot of things. Probably things he doesn't want to talk about." She heard his underlying accusation loud and clear, knowing that both he and her younger brother were still worried because she had never talked about her time over there. But she had no intention of getting into that with him right now.

"Well, there's got to be a connection to his time there. I just don't know how to make the dots all line up."

"What's your friend say?"

"He doesn't know how to make the dots line up either." She paused, weighing her thoughts carefully, knowing she had to watch every word she said to her brother. "I think that whoever's leaving these messages blames him for something that happened over there."

"Doesn't take a detective to figure that one out, CC."

"No, guess not." So much for being subtle. But she shouldn't be surprised. Bubby didn't do subtle. "Don't suppose there's a way to pull a list of patients, soldiers, he came in contact with over there."

"That would be one hell of a lot of names, CC. You'd be better off asking your friend if anything stuck out in his mind."

"Nothing does."

"I don't know what to tell you. And as for your oh-so-subtle question, don't ask, because it's not happening."

CC swallowed her disappointment. Not that she expected to hear anything different—even she knew something like that would be next to impossible to find. Not to mention that it would be a risk to Bubby if he started digging through so many files, classified or not.

"When are you coming home? Mom says she can't remember what you look like, it's been so long."

"Wow. Guilt trip, much? It hasn't been that long."

"Long enough. You should call her, let her know when you're coming down."

"I will. Maybe in a few weeks. I've got some vacation time I need to use up anyway."

"Hm. Do yourself a favor and don't phrase it like that when you talk to her, okay? And CC?"

"Yeah?"

"Just watch yourself."

"Always." She smiled into the phone then disconnected the call before her brother could make a sarcastic comeback. Because he would. As her big brother, he felt it was his familial duty to keep her firmly grounded, and he wielded sarcasm with an expert tongue.

She tucked the phone back into her pocket then stretched her legs out and tilted her head back, staring at nothing while her mind worked.

Her Big Guy was in trouble, only he didn't want to admit how much. Probably not even to himself. And whatever was going on had the potential of turning into, as they say, a real shit storm.

Any sane person would just walk away, as far and as fast as they could, putting as much distance as possible between them and potential trouble. She had just met Dave, there was no reason she shouldn't be hightailing it in the other direction already. She didn't really know him, certainly didn't owe him anything.

The phantom feel of his hand brushed against her calf, and she remembered the look on his face when he

had first touched the mangled flesh of her leg.
Concern, not repulsion. She wouldn't lie to herself and
say that something hadn't melted inside her at his
reaction.

Then there had been the sound of his laughter,
deep and rich as it drifted over her, the memory
warming her almost as much now as when she first
heard it. The sound had surprised her, so deep and rich,
a little rusty at the edges, like he didn't laugh often. And
something else had tugged and twisted and gotten all
soft inside her at the sound. She wanted to hear his
laughter again, see his full mouth lift into a real smile,
see that smile light up those dark eyes and chase away
the haunted shadows filling them.

It was such a girlie reaction, a need to comfort and
feel, so completely unlike her, that she snorted in
surprise.

So no, she wasn't going to hightail it anywhere—
unless it was straight back into his arms. For whatever
reason, she felt drawn to the Big Guy. And she hadn't
felt drawn to anybody in a long time.

No, she wasn't going anywhere, whether the
decision made sense or not.

Now she just had to convince the Big Guy that it
was for the best.

Chapter Nine

Cars and trucks filled the parking lot, leaving room for only those adventurous enough to squeeze into haphazard spaces that were nothing more than ruts on a slight incline.

Or for a daredevil spitfire on a motorcycle that had no concept of the term speed limit.

CC slid the bike into a small clearing at the far back corner of the lot and cut the engine. She reached up and pulled off the helmet, her long hair cascading in waves down her back as she shook her head. She looked over her shoulder and smiled.

"We need to take these roads in the daylight when I can really open it up."

Dave stared at her, afraid to open his mouth, afraid his voice would come out as nothing more than a squeak. He eased his white-knuckled grip from the seat and flexed his fingers, trying to get the blood flowing back into his hands.

"No, really. We don't." He pulled his own helmet off and swung one leg over the side, nearly stumbling.

CC pretended not to notice as she swung her own leg over the seat and set the kickstand.

How he let her talk him into this, he didn't know. She had shown up at his house two hours ago, unannounced. Granted, he had been thinking about her—had been doing little else, when he wasn't worrying about the messages, that is—but he was still surprised that she had just shown up.

They had talked a little, and then, before he realized it, they were on their way here, to Duffy's.

Because he had made the mistake of mentioning that this was where his shift had come tonight. No, he was adamant when he told her did not want to join them. He wasn't in the mood to socialize, wasn't in the mood to see his sister.

And yet here they were.

Dave still wasn't sure how that happened.

CC moved next to him and placed her hand in the center of his chest. Warmth instantly filled him at her touch. "Why do you look so confused, Big Guy?"

"I'm not confused."

"Hm. If you say so." She fisted her hand in his shirt and tugged, pulling him down until her mouth closed over his, hot, insistent, intoxicating. Dave groaned and snaked one arm around her waist, pulling her closer, his mouth feeding on her, his body already reacting to her nearness, to her touch.

She pulled away with a small groan, then tilted her head to the side and studied him. "Have you ever had sex on a motorcycle?"

"What?" Dave choked the answer, not believing she had just come right out and asked the question. "No. No, I haven't." Then he paused and looked at her, his eyes narrowed. "Have you?"

"Nope." She turned and studied the bike then looked back at him, her brows lowered in thought. "I think it's doable. Want to give it a try?"

"What? Here? Now?" Dave stepped back and shook his head. "I didn't just say that, and we're not having this conversation."

CC laughed and grabbed his hand then tugged him across the parking lot. "Don't worry, Big Guy, I was only joking. Sort of."

He pulled back, stopping her before they reached the door. "CC, this isn't a good idea. I haven't been here in months, and I'm really not in the mood—"

"Relax, it'll be fun."

"I don't think—"

She silenced him with another kiss, then leaned back and gave him a warm smile. "Tell you what. We'll give it an hour, and if you're still miserable, we can leave. Deal?"

Dave didn't have the chance to answer, because she just pulled him along until they were inside. The band was set up against the left wall, playing a nineties rock hit. The music was loud, upbeat, encouraging the crowd on the floor to dance. Those who weren't dancing were sitting or standing around the tables or bar, chatting or just watching.

CC paused just inside the door, standing on her toes to look around the crowd. Dave almost smiled, knowing there was no way she could see through the throng of people in front of her. Then he wondered what she was even looking for, since she didn't know anyone on his shift.

He tightened his grip on her hand and scanned the far wall, looking for everyone from work. Sure enough, there they were, in their usual spot tucked into the corner. He stepped in front of CC, intending to lead the way through the crowd, but stopped when she pulled on his arm.

"Let's go to the bar first. I want to get a drink."

"CC, I don't think—"

"C'mon, it won't be that bad." Then she pulled on his hand once more, pushing through the crowd until they reached the bar. And Dave wasn't sure how she did it, but she managed to find an empty spot, pushing between two guys until they made room for her.

CC gave them a smile then sat her helmet on the bar in front of her and leaned forward, looking around with curiosity. Dave's eyes scanned the bar area, coming to a stop on his sister. Surprise crossed her face when she noticed him, and he didn't know if that was a good thing or not. He wanted to smile, or nod, or something to acknowledge her presence, but he was frozen in place. He saw the other bartender, Rick, start toward them, noticed Angie stop him with a hand on his arm and a shake of her head.

She leaned over and said something to Rick before making her way over to them. Her gaze moved to CC, full of curiosity, then drifted back to him.

Dave guessed that was a good sign, that she was the one coming over to wait on them and not Rick. Unless Angie had plans to tell him off or read him the riot act or something like that.

But she didn't. In fact, she didn't say anything when she reached them. She just stood there, her gaze moving silently between CC and him. And he had no idea what to say, his mind going absolutely blank.

How sad was it that he didn't even know what to say to his own sister?

But CC didn't have that problem, just jumped

right in with a huge smile and friendly voice. "I'm CC. And you just have to be Dave's sister, Angie. I'd recognize the similarity anywhere."

Dave coughed, surprised at the thickened drawl in CC's voice, surprised at how sure and sincere she sounded.

Because he was pretty sure he and Angie didn't resemble one another, not in any way that would be obvious to a complete stranger. From the brief glance she flickered at him, a similar thought must have gone through Angie's mind as well. But she merely smiled and shook CC's offered hand, not saying anything.

In fact, none of them said anything amid the noise of the crowd and the music around them. Dave squirmed, feeling suddenly as uncomfortable as his sister looked in the awkward silence.

Then an elbow nudged him in the stomach, hard enough to cause his breath to leave him. He grabbed his side and looked down at CC, only to see her giving him a meaningful look with her wide eyes.

"Big Guy, don't be rude. Say hello to your sister."

Dave rubbed his side, taking a deep breath. Damn, he hadn't expected her to actually hit him like that. And he hadn't expected it to hurt, either. He looked down at CC, his eyes narrowed, only to see her roll her eyes. She reached out and patted his side.

"Oh please, I didn't hit you that hard. Besides, I'll kiss it later and make it better. Now go on, be nice and say hello to your sister."

He looked up and saw Angie watching them in surprise, one hand covering her mouth. If he didn't know better, he'd swear she was trying to hide a smile. Seeing that made a little of his tension disappeared. Not all of it, just enough that he didn't feel quite so much like a stranger to his sister. He tried to smile at her, the move stiff on his lips, and saw a flicker of something in Angie's dark eyes. And he realized that they were his eyes.

Why the hell had he never realized that before?

"Hey Angie. You, uh, you look good."

"Oh. Thanks." Her eyes slid away from his, toward CC and back again. "You, uh, you look...well, actually, you look like hell."

CC's sudden laughter did nothing to keep the scowl from Dave's face. He looked around, noticed the curious glances from the nearby patrons, then turned back. Angie and CC both were still smiling, ignoring the looks they were receiving from everyone else.

Ignoring Dave's scowl.

"I think I like you, Angie. Who knows, maybe we'll even be friends."

A very small part of Dave was gratified to see that his sister was taken completely off-guard. Angie watched CC for a long second, a half-smile on her face that didn't quite hide the confusion in her eyes. Then she turned to face him, her silent question loud and clear as it passed between them.

Who is this woman?

And under that, concern. Concern for whatever she thought she had seen in his face to make her think he looked awful. And maybe even concern about the woman standing next to him.

Dave wanted to assure her that CC wasn't quite as crazy as she seemed, that she was safe. For crying out loud, she was a cop. But he didn't think it was exactly protocol to be advertising that fact in a bar full of strangers.

So he just tried to smile at her again and silently

reassure his sister that everything was fine.

CC nudged him again, not hard this time, then reached out and took the helmet from his hand. She placed it next to hers, then pushed both of them toward his sister. "Angie, would you mind putting these back there somewhere? I'm not sure how much room there's going to be at the table, and I don't want anything happening to them. I don't mind so much for myself, but Big Guy here won't ride the motorcycle without one."

"Motorcycle? Dave?" Angie stopped, one hand on each helmet, and looked at him with wide, disbelieving eyes. She blinked, shook her head, then turned to CC. "Dave, my brother, drove a motorcycle here?"

"Of course not, silly. I like him, but nobody drives my bike. He rode with me."

Angie's eyes widened even more, surprise clear on her face. "Your bike? So he rode here, with you. On a motorcycle. Dave. This guy right here?"

Dave clenched his jaw, irritation blooming within him. Did Angie really have to look so surprised? And did she really have to talk about him like he wasn't even here? He opened his mouth to say something, then immediately shut it when CC moved to stand next to him, sliding her hand up to the middle of his chest. Her other hand grabbed his and squeezed. Hard.

"Absolutely he did. Your brother is just full of surprises. Aren't you, Big Guy?" And then she stood on her toes and kissed him. Not a quick meeting of the lips, but a full, mouth-on-mouth, tongue-dueling kiss that made him momentarily forget where he was.

Until he heard a few cheers and whistles from the handful of people standing around them.

CC slowly pulled away, giving him a quick wink

103

before she turned back to the bar. And Dave was pretty sure that the stunned surprise on Angie's face was a mirror of his own.

"Whenever you get the chance, Angie, could you be a dear and get us two beers? We're going to go dance." CC tugged on his hand and led him straight into the crowd, pushing people out of the way until she claimed a spot on the dance floor. The crowd had thinned out, leaving room for couples to sway to the slow song that was just starting.

CC stepped into Dave's arms, one hand resting high on his chest, the other on his hip. She shook a few thick strands of hair out of her face, then looked up at him with a smile. He cleared his throat and finally found his voice.

"What the hell was all that about?"

"All what?"

"That whole drawn-out southern belle thing you had going on back there."

"Oh, that." CC laughed, then looked up and batted her eyelashes at him. "Poor little old me. Maybe I should've added a few 'y'alls' and 'bless your hearts' while I was at it. Would that have been better?"

"I'm not sure, considering you don't look the part."

"Are you saying you don't like what I have on? Well, thanks. There goes my ego."

Dave tightened his arms around her and pulled her closer. "No, I happen to like your outfit quite a bit."

And he did. Her black jeans hugged her curves, making his palms itch to run over each inch of her legs. Her blouse was made from some billowy, flowing material, cut just low enough to showcase the full cleavage of her rounded breasts. The material was a shimmering forest green that reflected in her hazel eyes, turning them a unique shade he couldn't quite identify.

But what he really liked was her leather jacket, with its plain buckles and squared collar. The buttery soft material hugged her curves and nipped in at her waist, showcasing every womanly inch of her body.

He had been having fantasies about her in just the leather jacket during the entire ride over here, despite being worried she was going to send them both crashing to the asphalt.

"You didn't hear a word I just said."

Dave blinked and looked down, only to find CC smiling up at him. "I'm sorry. What?"

"Never mind. If that look in your eyes means what I hope it means, I'll forgive you and let you make it up to me later." She leaned forward and placed a kiss in the open V of his shirt, kicking his pulse up a notch. "What I was saying, when you were so adorably zoned out staring at my chest, was that I liked your sister. She's worried about you."

Dave opened his mouth to argue that he hadn't been staring at her chest, then snapped it shut again, thinking it was probably better not to say anything at all. CC grinned at him, but he chose to ignore it. "And why do you think she's worried about me?"

"Because of the concerned looks she was giving you, and that whole silent communication thing you two had going on. Like she was asking who I was."

"I think you're reading too much—"

"And I'll bet you a full body massage that she comes over to talk to you at some point tonight. Deal?"

"You're wrong."

"Then you don't have anything to lose. Full body

massage. Naked. With oil. Is it a bet?"

"I don't have any oil."

"Then I guess it's a good thing I brought some with me, isn't it?"

Dave froze on the dance floor, his body immediately jumping to attention. And from the sly grin on CC's face, she knew it, too. But then the song ended and she stepped away from him, her smile growing wider.

"Why don't you go sit with your friends, and I'll go get our drinks and meet you over there."

"No, I'll go with you. You don't know where they're sitting."

"Yeah I do. Back corner tables, just over my left shoulder."

"How'd you know that?"

"Because they've been watching us ever since we walked in." She leaned up and gave him a quick kiss then stepped around him, swatting his ass as she walked by.

She swatted his ass. On the dance floor. In front of everyone.

Dave looked over and sure enough, every single one of his co-workers was watching him. Their looks ranged from speculation to amusement to laughing curiosity. Great. Now he'd have to listen to everyone's questions and lewd comments, of that he had no doubt.

Chapter Ten

He glanced over his shoulder and watched as CC made her way to the bar, leaning over it and saying something to Angie. His sister glanced over at him, too far away for him to make out the expression in her eyes. But she smiled, so he smiled back. Then, taking a deep breath, he turned and made his way over to the far corner.

"Well look who decided to join us. Have a seat." Pete grinned and pulled out a chair, motioning for Dave to sit.

"Are you out of your snit now?"

"Who is she?"

"You never said you were dating anyone."

"About time you came over to join us."

Dave lowered himself into the chair then turned it slightly sideways, so he could talk to everyone and watch the bar at the same time.

"I haven't been in a snit, I've just had a lot on my mind. And I'll introduce you when she gets over here." Dave ignored the assorted groans and complaints as his gaze drifted around the table, finally stopping on Jay Moore—the firefighter from his shift that Angie was dating. The man met his gaze with a slight nod, but didn't say anything.

And for a few quiet seconds, strained silence fell over everyone around them. Dave realized, with a sickening clarity that disturbed him, that this tense silence had permeated work for the last several months.

Ever since Angie and Jay had started dating again. Ever since his baby sister had moved out because he couldn't deal with it.

Had he really been that much of an ass? And as much as he might want to, he couldn't blame his entire reaction on worry over the messages he had been receiving. No, it was more basic than that. He had refused to admit his sister was a grown woman, that she was old enough and responsible enough and mature enough to make her own decisions.

And, for some reason, she had decided to date one of the guys he worked with. Not just date, but move in with, if the quiet conversations he wasn't supposed to overhear at work meant anything.

Jay, who had never had a serious relationship that lasted more than a week in the entire time Dave had known him.

Jay, who looked happier than he had ever seen him in the more than six months he had been seeing Angie.

Damn, he really was an asshole. Why hadn't he seen any of this before? Why had he almost destroyed his relationship with his sister over this? Almost destroyed his friendship with the man sitting across from him, a look of wariness on his face?

Dave nodded, just a quick acknowledgement. "Jay. Good to see you."

The tense silence lifted and everyone began talking again, but Dave ignored them, his eyes still on Jay. The man he had formerly called friend finally nodded and lifted his bottle in an informal salute, his mouth turning up in a small grin.

Silence once again settled over the table, different this time, full of expectation. Dave turned his head, not surprised to see CC approaching the table with two bottles of beer and a huge smile.

Conversation erupted again, and Pete even jumped out of his chair, pushing it toward CC with a broad smile.

"Well aren't you so nice. But I already have a seat, thank you." And she stepped around Pete and sat right on Dave's lap, straddling his right leg and settling her deliciously round ass right up against his groin. She shifted, getting comfortable, then turned and handed him one of the bottles.

"Well aren't you going to introduce me, Big Guy?"

She wiggled her ass again and he had to smother a groan, knowing she was deliberately trying to get a rise out of him. Literally.

And it was working.

He briefly narrowed his eyes at her, then took a swallow of the beer, which only made her laugh. He wrapped one arm around her waist and held her tight so she would stop moving, then pointed at everyone around the table, introducing them one by one.

"This is Pete Miller, he's our Lieutenant. Next to him is Dale Gannon, the engine driver. That's Jimmy Hughes, my partner."

Jimmy nodded his head and smiled, showing a

dimple. If Dave could have kicked him, he would. "Ma'am."

"Well aren't you just the sweetest." CC turned her head and smiled at Dave, amusement flashing in her eyes as she rolled them just the tiniest bit. "Isn't he sweet? He just called me ma'am."

Dave choked back his laughter and motioned again with his bottle. "That's Mikey Donaldson. One of the fireman on our shift. Nick, the band's lead singer, is her fiancé."

"Short for Michelle?"

"Actually, it's Michaela. Nice seeing you again."

Dave grinned when five heads turned to look at Mike in confusion. He saw CC acknowledge Mikey's observation with a smile and small nod, but neither woman said anything else. And if they weren't going to say anything, neither was he.

"This is Jay Moore, another fireman."

"Oh. You're the one who's dating Angie." CC tilted her head, her clear eyes studying Jay so intently that the man squirmed. A secret sense of satisfaction went through Dave when he noticed it, until CC turned that intensity on him. "I don't know why you're so upset. They make a cute couple. I think they'll do well together."

"See? See? I told you they were cute together!" Pete spread his arms wide and grinned at the entire table. Mikey groaned and tossed a coaster at him, hitting him square in the chest.

"Pete, how many times do I have to tell you? You're a moron."

Laughter erupted when Pete looked around, silently asking what it was he had done. Dave ignored him, continuing with the introductions. When he was finished, CC nodded at each person again, repeating their names as she acknowledged each one. Dave didn't bother to hide the fact that he was impressed.

Jimmy leaned forward, smiling so broadly his dimple showed again. "So how do you and Mike know each other?"

"Oh, we don't know each other. I just met her."

"But—" Jimmy paused, looking between the two women. "She said it was nice meeting you *again*. So when did you two meet?"

CC looked over her shoulder and grinned at him, then turned back in his lap and leaned closer to the table. Dave noticed Jimmy's eyes glance down, knew he was peeking down CC's blouse. He suddenly wanted to reach across the table and grab him by the throat. CC must have picked up on it, though, because she kicked the instep of his foot with one of her booted feet. Then she leaned across the table even more and smiled at Jimmy.

"Well, it was the same night we met, silly."

Jimmy tilted his head, still smiling, but obviously not understanding. "No, we've never met. I'd definitely remember that."

"Of course we did. Almost two weeks ago."

"Two weeks ago?"

"Now see, you've gone and hurt my feelings. I was sure you'd remember me."

"No. There's no way we met." Jimmy leaned forward a little more, enough that the back legs of his chair lifted off the floor. He was still smiling, but confusion filled his eyes as he obviously tried to remember when they could have possibly met.

Dave saw CC and Mikey exchange a glance and he almost felt sorry for Jimmy, because he knew what was coming. Almost. But he still wanted to grab him around the throat because Jimmy's eyes drifted down again, staring straight down CC's blouse. Mikey leaned over and gently nudged him in the side, but Jimmy's gaze didn't move.

"Jimmy! Remember that ATV accident we had? This is the Flight Medic. She was the one on scene when we flew him out. She's a cop."

Laughter erupted when realization finally dawned on Jimmy. His mouth opened in surprise and he jerked back like he had been hit. His chair flew out from under him, sending him sprawling to the floor, his beer splashing down on top of him. Dave leaned down, peering under the table to see Jimmy slumped in a graceless heap on the floor.

"You had that one coming. *Partner.*"

The laughter grew louder as Jimmy groaned then finally pulled himself up. He righted his chair and sat down, using the napkins Jay handed him to wipe at his shirt.

CC leaned back and reached down for Dave's hand, threading her fingers with his and squeezing. He tightened his arm around her waist, holding her close, surprised at how normal everything felt.

Normal. And right. Like he was almost himself again.

He raised the bottle to his mouth then paused when he noticed CC grinning at him. "What?"

"I think your sister wants to talk to you."

"What?" Dave looked past their table and sure enough, here came Angie. He didn't think anything of it, figuring she was coming to see Jay. His assumption was proved correct when she leaned down and gave Jay a quick kiss.

Then she straightened, glanced briefly at CC, then looked right at him.

"Dave, could I see you for a minute?"

CC scooted off his lap, a broad smile on her face as he reluctantly stood. She swatted him on the ass, again, and laughed as everyone watched them.

"I just can't wait for that full body massage later tonight."

Dave walked away, laughter ringing behind him as his face heated in embarrassment. He was just glad nobody could see exactly how her parting comment had affected him.

Chapter Eleven

Angie led him around the bar then kept going, not saying a word as she pushed through the door to the back room. She kept going, her stride purposeful as she moved through a short narrow hallway filled with boxes that ended at another door. She turned sideways and pushed it with her hip, holding it open for him.

Dave walked out into the cool night air, turning as Angie propped the door open with a small block wedge. She finally faced him, her dark eyes studying him with curiosity.

The silence around them wasn't quite uncomfortable, but not exactly warm and comforting. Dave shifted, looking around at the pile of broken-down cardboard next to the dumpster, the aging bench pushed against the outside wall, the old painter's bucket filled with sand someone had been using as an ashtray. The music was muted out here, slightly muffled, not quite as loud. The spot was somewhat secluded, offering a certain amount of privacy, the surroundings quiet enough to have a conversation without the need for shouting.

Except Dave had no idea what to say. And he had the impression that Angie wasn't quite sure what to say, either. She stood just outside the door, her arms folded across her chest, her dark hair framing her oval face as she studied him. She moved her hands up and down her arms, like she was trying to warm herself, only it wasn't quite cold enough for that.

Disappointment and sorrow filled him, creating an ache deep in his chest. The woman standing mere feet away from him was his sister, his own flesh-and-blood. He'd been looking out for her for years, watching her grow as he struggled to be a big brother while takin on the role of father at the same time. They'd been through so much together. It shouldn't be this hard to find something to say, for either one of them.

And then he realized that he hadn't spoken to her in months, not since that night back in June when she came home from the camping trip.

The trip where he had abandoned her, left her behind in a fit of childish temper. All because she had chosen something that made her happy.

Dave swallowed against the lump of guilt clogging his throat, wondering if he could ever make it up to her. If they could ever go back to the way things were. She was his sister, dammit. It shouldn't be this hard.

He opened his mouth, closed it, shook his head. Angie looked over at him, her teeth pulling on her lower lip, then dropped her gaze to the dust and gravel under her feet. Dave took a deep breath and let it out, tried to smile.

"How's school? You keeping up with all your studies?"

Angie's gaze lifted back to his, her eyes cautious as she nodded. "Yes. Yeah, everything's good. I think Doc Cassidy is going to bring me on full-time when I finish in the spring."

"Hey, that's great. Congratulations, kiddo." Dave saw her wince, just the barest movement, when he called her 'kiddo'. He jammed his hands in his front pockets and sighed. "I'm, uh, probably going to always call you 'kiddo', you know? I don't really mean it like you take it."

Angie looked at him, both eyebrows raised in surprise—or maybe doubt—as one corner of her mouth tilted up in a hesitant smile. But she didn't say anything.

Dave shifted, even more uncomfortable, wishing there was a way to erase the damage he had done, wishing there was a way he could just make everything right again. He knew Angie had asked him out here for a reason, had thought she was going to grill him about CC. But now that they were out here, she didn't seem anxious to ask him about anything.

He could ask her what she wanted, just answer whatever questions she may have and leave it at that. But that would be the easy thing to do, and it would do nothing to heal the rift between them.

"Shit." He muttered the word and ran one hand over his face. Angie looked over at him, confusion clear on his face. Confusion, and something that resembled caution, like she expected him to lecture her or yell at her or something like that. And he hated seeing that expression on her face, in her eyes.

He closed the distance between them and yanked her into a hard hug. She held herself stiffly for a few seconds, no doubt surprised, probably confused and taken completely off-guard. Then her arms came around his waist, hesitant at first before finally tightening, hugging him back.

"I'm sorry, Angie. For everything. So sorry." Dave's voice was gruff, embarrassing him, but he didn't pull away. And he didn't say anything else, even though there was so much else to say. He just didn't know how.

Angie mumbled something, the words muffled against his chest. Her arms tightened a bit more around his waist then eased, and Dave felt her trying to pull back. But he didn't want to let her go, not just yet, not when he hoped his hug was saying all the things he couldn't quite put into words.

"You're squishing me."

Dave finally heard the words, muttered on a small wheeze, and he jumped back, surprised. He looked down at Angie, saw the slight smile on her face when she stepped away. She turned her head and brushed her face against her shoulder, her eyes still bright with moisture as she laughed. Not a full laugh, more like a surprised exhale.

But he'd take it, knowing—hoping—it was a start.

"Since when do you get all mushy?"

"I'm not mushy. What? I can't give my sister a hug and say I'm sorry for being an ass?"

Angie smiled up at him, a little more at ease, then threw her arms around him once more and hugged him so hard he felt his breath leave him in a small gasp. Then she pulled away and sat down on the bench, patting the space beside her. "I'm sorry, too."

Dave sat next to her, turning so they were face-to-face. "What are you sorry for?"

"I should have told you. When Jay and I first started dating, I mean. I shouldn't have tried to hide it."

"Ang, don't. I didn't exactly make it easy for you. I know that." Silence settled around them once more, not quite as uncomfortable as before. Dave shifted on the bench, looked down and took a deep breath, looked back at Angie. "So. Are things working out? You happy?"

"Yeah, I am." She paused, chewing on her lower lip like she was trying to decide what to say. "Jay bought a townhouse. North of Cockeysville."

"Yeah, I heard something like that at work."

She paused, picking at the material of her jeans, then watched him from the corner of her eye. "He, uh, asked me to move in with him."

Her announcement wasn't exactly news to him. He had heard the quiet conversations at work, caught more than everyone thought he did, even though everybody had been careful about what they said near him. But he still felt a flash of protectiveness, of concern, when Angie said the words out loud. His first instinct was to tell her no, she was too young to be shacking up with anyone, too young to be getting so serious.

But she wasn't too young. And it hadn't been a question. So Dave took a deep breath and did his best to unclench his fists before speaking. "Are you?"

Angie smiled, happiness lighting her eyes. "Yeah, I think so."

A hundred different things went through Dave's mind, a hundred different things that wanted to tumble from his mouth. But none of them were the right thing to say. So he took another deep breath and let it out slowly, tried to give her a smile. "Well then, let me know if you need any help moving."

"You mean it?"

"Yeah." Dave cleared his throat, then frowned at her. "But the first time I hear he makes you unhappy, I'm kicking his ass."

Angie laughed and leaned forward, giving him a brief hug. He patted her back, just a little awkwardly, then watched her as she sat back and pulled one knee to her chest. There was a mischievous glint in her dark eyes as she studied him.

"Okay, fess up. Who is she?"

"Who?"

"Really? Don't play that game, you know who. Now tell me all about her. Where did you meet? How long have you been dating her?"

Dave looked away, not knowing what to say. And not knowing how to answer the dating question. Were they dating? Well, he was sleeping with her. Did that count? Not that he was about to tell his kid sister that.

"I met her through work. She's a flight medic."

"She's a cop? Seriously? Oh my God, I would have never thought that. She's too cute to be a cop."

Dave actually cringed, knowing CC would have laughed at hearing the description. Knowing that part of her enjoyed using that perception to her advantage. And it was slightly unsettling for him to realize that he knew that, so soon after meeting her.

He didn't have a chance to respond, because the back door opened and Jay poked his head out. Concern creased his forehead as he looked over at them, obviously worried they might be arguing. Dave clenched his jaw at the look but didn't say anything, knowing he probably would have done the same.

"Hey Ang, band's getting ready to take a break, they need us behind the bar."

"Us? Since when do you work here?"

Angie bounced from the bench and squeezed his shoulder. "He doesn't. He just likes to keep me company when we get busy."

Dave stood up, ready to follow them back in, when Angie stopped and faced him again. She smiled, then gave him another hug, quick and hard.

"Thanks Dave. I missed you."

He stood there for a second, surprised at the quick hug, then closed his arms around her again. "Missed you, too, kiddo."

Angie stepped back then turned on her heel and walked through the door. Dave expected Jay to follow her, but he didn't. Instead, he stood there, his hand holding the door open, his steel-gray eyes cool as he studied Dave.

"I'm glad you guys seem to be getting along again. Things back to normal?"

"Maybe." Dave stepped through the door then turned to face Jay. "That doesn't mean I won't kick your ass if you hurt her, Moore."

"I'm not planning on it."

"Good. That's good."

The two of them stood there in the short hallway, staring at each other, the challenge clear between them. Jay finally nodded, the motion short and quick, before he grinned. "Good. I, uh, I have to go help. And you might want to get back to the table, because Jimmy's trying to flirt with your girlfriend."

Jay walked up the hallway and pushed through the swinging door leading to the bar, leaving Dave to stare after him.

CC wasn't his girlfriend.

Was she?

Dave realized it didn't matter, because he was still

going to grab Jimmy by the throat when he got back out there.

If CC hadn't already done just that.

Chapter Twelve

Strains of soft music floated through the air, relaxing, soothing. Candlelight flickered from the nightstand and dresser, scenting the room with hints of vanilla and something just a little spicy, something CC couldn't quite make out.

She hadn't figured Big Guy to be a candles-and-classical music kind of guy. It didn't matter that she had subtly suggested some music and candlelight. Well, maybe not so subtly. But he had taken her suggestion to heart, and she was surprised at the music choice when he turned on the small stereo in his room.

Surprised, but certainly not complaining. Right now, she was certain that even annoying techno-music wouldn't grate on her nerves, not when Dave's large hands were gliding over her body, his touch strong, soothing, relaxing.

Big Guy definitely had magic hands.

And she had to give him credit for following through on the bet. Granted, he had looked a little surprised when she pulled the massage oil from the small overnight bag she had stored in the saddlebag on her bike. Well, maybe the surprise was from seeing her pull out an overnight bag to begin with. But he didn't say anything, just kind of grunted and led her into his house.

She hadn't wasted time reminding him that he lost the bet. And she was due for a full body massage. Then she had climbed the stairs and found his room, stripped down, tossed him the massage oil, then sprawled face down on his bed.

And waited.

At least he caught on quick.

His hands paused in the middle of her lower back, just above the towel he had tossed over her bare ass.

Because he said he couldn't concentrate if he didn't cover her up.

CC turned her head into the pillow, trying to hide her smile as his hands hesitated, and she knew he was debating whether or not to move the towel. He lifted his hands from her back, then moved them to the tops of her thighs, just under the edge of the towel.

"That's cheating, Big Guy."

He grunted again, his hands sliding along her thigh, his thumbs kneading the muscles with long, deep strokes. CC exhaled slowly, her body melting even more under his touch.

"Good?"

"Hmm. Amazing." She sighed again and closed her eyes as his hands drifted down her leg to her calf, not hesitating, not pausing.

Like he didn't care that most of her calf was missing, like he didn't even notice it. Another part of her melted, that tiny part locked in a secret corner that she didn't even want to admit existed.

There was no way he could know how much that meant to her, how much his wordless acceptance warmed a piece of her she hadn't admitted needed reassurance.

His hands drifted down to her foot, pressing, squeezing before he stopped. He reached over her and she heard him squeeze more oil into his palm, heard the whisper of skin on skin as he warmed it between his hands before starting on her other leg. She sighed again, reveling in the heat of his hands, the strength of his touch.

"Roll over." His words were a husky command. She sighed, every muscle in her body relaxed as she tried to push up with her hands, to find the strength to do as he asked. His hands reached up and grabbed her shoulder, rolling her as she grabbed hold of the headboard for leverage to move.

She moved, planning on bringing her arms to her side, but stopped when he shook his head.

"No. Don't move." His dark eyes were intense, filled with a deep hunger as they grazed her body. They lingered on her breasts, thrust upward by the stretch of her arms above her head.

CC smiled, a slow sultry smile as she shifted just a bit, her hands closing more firmly on the headboard. "Like this?"

"Hm. Just like that."

He straddled her hips, the heaviness of his thick erection a drooling enticement as he leaned over her and grabbed the massage oil. He held the bottle more than a foot above her, tilting it until a fine stream of oil spilled out, drizzling over her chest, down her stomach. CC's breath hitched in her chest at the coolness of the oil against her skin, at the slide of the oil against her flesh as it ran over her nipples and down the side of her breasts.

Desire burned in Dave's eyes as he watched her, watched the trail of oil travel across her body. He reached down with one finger, traced the line of oil from her neck to her right breast, the short nail of his finger grazing the tight peak of her nipple. She sucked her breath in on a hiss, moved her hand to touch him.

His free hand shot out and grabbed her wrist, led it back to the headboard. "Don't move." He leaned down, nipped at her earlobe. "Or I'll have to get your handcuffs."

CC swallowed and groaned, desire instantly searing her as moisture pooled between her legs. Dave leaned back and grinned, his expression wicked, promising. She groaned again and tightened her hand around the headboard as he drew the tip of his finger down her neck, across to her other breast, across her nipple.

He shifted his body, sliding down so he straddled her thighs, the strength of his legs keeping her own closed. She tilted her head and watched as he brought his hands together and fanned them low across her stomach, his thumbs dipping lower, teasing her with the faintest of touches before he leaned forward. His hands drifted up, spreading at the base of her ribcage, up further, slowly, cupping the fullness of each breast in his hand. His hips dipped, just enough that the head of his cock slipped between her closed legs, torturing her, teasing her, making her back arch in need.

"Dave."

He moved his hips again, pulling away. "I said don't move."

CC groaned, biting her lip as his hands moved

over her, slick and warm from the oil, from his own heat. Everywhere he touched, fire burned. Her stomach, her sides, her neck. He dragged his hands back down, closing over her breasts once more, squeezing, his thumbs teasing the tips of her nipples, turning the peaks harder.

Her head dropped back and she clenched her jaw, needing to move, needing to open her legs, needing him inside her. Now.

But his legs tightened even more around hers, imprisoning her as his hands continued their exploration, their torture. He shifted again, moving his hips, sliding up until he straddled her chest. His hands drifted to the sides of her breasts, pushing them together, and she felt the warm slide of his cock between them, slick with oil.

She opened her eyes and watched, licked her lips as his hands tightened around her breasts, holding them closer, his cock sliding in and out. Wetness coated her, desire thick, needy, pooling between her legs as her hips thrust under him.

Her eyes traveled up his body, over the muscles bunched in his arms, over the broad, muscular chest, sculpted by the hand of a master artist. Up to his throat, the pulse beat heavy and throbbing at the base. To his eyes, focused on her, dark with desire, sharp with need as he watched.

Watched her.

Watched the slide of his heavy cock between her breasts.

Her hands tightened against the headboard, so tight she could feel the wood digging into her fingers. She closed her eyes and let her head fall back, her hips searching, mimicking each thrust of his own.

Flames licked her, tongues of fire dancing across her skin with each slide of his cock. Her hips thrust again as desire coiled tightly inside her, tighter, pulling, promising.

The climax crashed over her, surprising her with its arrival, with its intensity. Her back arched and she screamed Dave's name through clenched teeth, her body bucking beneath his.

He slid down her body, his strong hands spreading her legs and pulling them against his chest as he drove into her. His thick length pierced her, filling her, shattering her again and again. Her head tossed from side to side, her breathing ragged, harsh, short as he thrust into her, again and again.

Hard. Deep. Fast.

And suddenly it was too much, the sensation, the shattering. She screamed again and arched off the bed, her hands leaving the headboard and reaching down for him, needing to feel him, touch him.

Her fingers dug into his thighs, the corded muscle hard as steel under her touch. Waves continued to crash over her, molten lava, burning. Her nails raked his skin, it was too much, not enough, she wanted more, needed to feel him.

A deep growl, feral, needy, echoed around them. Dave's hands tightened around her legs, his hips pumping, his head thrown back as he spilled himself inside her.

Her fingers relaxed against his legs, her heart sliding back into her chest as his harsh breathing, their breathing, filled the room, drowning out all other sound.

Seconds ticked by as the last shudders drifted across her body, finally stilling. She took a deep breath, then another, trying to draw air into her lungs as Dave shifted. His hold on her legs gentled and he kissed the inside of her thigh, then gently eased her legs down to the bed. He shuddered once more then stretched out on top of her, his mouth hot on hers. He pulled away, his eyes still intense despite the small grin on his face. She returned the smile and reached up to touch his face, her fingers drifting into his hair.

"Wow." Her voice was hoarse, scratchy. Dave's grin widened and he leaned down, pressing a quick kiss against her lips. He dropped his forehead against hers and sighed as she ran her hands over his back, reveling in the bunching of muscles as she caressed him.

He shifted, his arms shaking slightly, then rolled to the side, draping his arm and leg over her and pulling her close. His mouth grazed the side of her neck, his teeth nipping at the sensitive spot between her neck and shoulder, sending another shudder through her.

"I think that's the best bet I ever lost." His breath was warm against her skin, the smile in his words warming her inside. She shifted and rolled the tiniest bit, just so she could look at him. She reached up and traced the outline of his lips with the tip of one finger, marveling at their soft fullness on a man so big.

"Anytime you're ready to lose another one, Big Guy, just let me know."

He nipped her finger then reached out and tucked her head against his chest, his hand drawing lazy circles on her back. "I think I need a day to recuperate first. After that, you're on."

She laughed, then snuggled closer, the steady beat of his heart lulling her, pulling her into the grayness of slumber. CC blinked and shook it off, lifting her head so she could look down at him. His eyes were closed, his lashes long and dark against his skin.

"What are you doing next week?"

"Hm?" He opened his eyes and looked at her, his gaze sleepy and content. "This week coming up, or next?"

"Next."

He closed his eyes, his lips moving silently for a second, then opened them again. "Night work Monday and Tuesday. Why?"

"Can you take off?"

"Probably, if the calendar isn't full. Why?"

CC leaned over and pressed a kiss to his chin, then dropped her head back to his chest. She wasn't sure what had prompted her to ask, but now that she had, she felt shy about asking.

"Why?" Dave repeated the question, his hand tightening just a bit on her shoulder.

CC shrugged, still not looking at him, then let out a deep breath. "I have to run down home for a quick visit and was wondering if you wanted to go. No biggie if you don't, I know it's short notice and all."

Dave's hand drifted across her back then curled under her chin, turning her head so she was looking at him. He leaned forward and pressed a kiss against her temple then smiled.

"I'd love to."

CC smiled then dropped her head back to his chest. She had nearly drifted off when he spoke one last time, his voice thick with sleep.

"But we're not taking the motorcycle."

Chapter Thirteen

He heard the crunch-pop under the sole of his boot at the same time he felt the small piece of trash slide under his foot. He cursed and stepped back, looking down at what was left of a piece of granola bar smashed on the floor of the medic.

"Dammit."

Dave shoved the trash he was holding into the small plastic bag, then grabbed a gauze pad from the cabinet. It didn't come close to being a thorough cleaning job, but at least it was a start, something to do as he waited for Jimmy to come out. Then they'd give it a thorough cleaning, starting with a full sweeping.

Correction. Jimmy could sweep it out. Not because the mess was his fault. No, he'd stick his partner with the cleaning as payback for last weekend at Duffy's.

It wasn't the worse payback around, but it was a good start. And as much as he'd love to blame Jimmy for the mess, he knew he couldn't. Their last patient had been a hoarder, to the extent that his pockets had been filled with all sorts of food.

His pockets, his socks, even his underwear.

The thought made Dave seriously consider giving up eating. Forever.

Or at least until dinner.

He glanced around, seeing if he had missed anything else, then tied the trash bag and jumped out of the medic, slamming the door behind him. It shouldn't have been as trashed as it was, not for a simple chest pain call.

But the patient hadn't appreciated it when Jimmy tried to unbutton his shirt to place the monitor leads on his chest. The two of them had tussled, until the patient's stash had gone flying all over the back of the medic.

And most of the food hadn't been wrapped.

Dave muttered to himself then walked through the ER entrance, tossing the bag into the large trashcan as he walked by. His skin still felt like it was crawling and he resisted the urge to scratch, knowing that the itching was purely in his head.

So far, it had been a pretty interesting Sunday. But his shift was over in less than two hours. And about twelve hours after that, he'd be leaving with CC, heading down to South Carolina.

As soon as he found Jimmy, they could finish wiping down the medic, get back to the station. And then, soon, he could head home.

He couldn't remember the last time he had been so eager to get home.

"You look like the cat that ate the proverbial canary."

"Hm?" He looked up to see Jimmy walking down the hall toward him, clipboard dangling by his side. "I do?"

"Yeah, you do. You've got this shit-eating grin on your face. I'm not used to seeing it."

"Well, maybe you better get used to seeing it."

"Wouldn't have anything to do with a certain Flight Medic and you taking off night trick, would it?"

"Like I'd tell you if it did."

Jimmy pounded him on the back and laughed. "And you call yourself my partner. I'd tell you if there was anything interesting going on."

Dave looked over at him, then glanced down the hall to the triage desk. He shook his head, trying not to smile. "And since you're not, I can only guess that Sheila turned you down. Again."

"Hey, she's warming up to me. Eventually she'll say yes."

Dave didn't bother reminding Jimmy that nobody took him seriously, not with the way he flirted with every nurse here. His chance of getting any of them to say yes was slim.

They walked back outside and climbed into the medic, starting the process of cleaning and wiping everything down after Jimmy cleaned the floor. They used disinfectant on all the surfaces. More than once.

Jimmy tossed the last of the rags into a trash bag then looked over at Dave, his expression serious. "I want you to promise me something. As my partner."

Dave turned and watched him, his gaze skeptical and hesitant. "Depends. What is it?"

"Don't ever let me get like that old guy. Hoarding everything, afraid to let anything go. I can't imagine living like that, all alone with nothing but stuff."

"Jimmy, if you ever become a hoarder, I will personally make sure you're buried under your piles of possessions before you reach old age. Will that work?"

"You're cold, Dave. Real cold. I'm going to go dump this. Grab your phone, I hear it vibrating up front."

Dave shook his head at Jimmy's pout—and his keen hearing—then walked to the front of the medic and climbed into the passenger seat. He leaned over, searching through the center console until his hand closed over the phone. The thing vibrated in his hand and he turned it over, looking at the screen.

And felt his gut clench in anger at the text message.

I know what you did. Time is drawing closer.

His fingers tightened around the phone and he had the urge to throw it out the window, or smash it against the concrete.

But he didn't. He didn't do anything except stare at the message.

Nearly a month had passed since the incident at CC's house, and nothing had happened since then. No more texts, no more mysterious notes left behind. And he had started to relax, to think that they had stopped again.

That they had stopped for good.

But it had just been another false lull, a brief break, long enough for him to forget about them. And now here was another one, hurtling him back to reality. Only this one was different, vaguely more threatening.

Time is drawing closer.

Anger rushed through him and he clenched his jaw as he stared at the message. He was ready for this to end, ready to find out who was behind it, ready to put a stop to it.

"Then bring it on, you son of a bitch."

"What?"

Dave looked up as Jimmy climbed into the medic, then tucked the phone into his pocket and shook his head. "Nothing, I was just talking to myself."

Jimmy nodded and started the engine, then glanced over and grinned at him. "You know that's a sign of old age, right?"

Dave flipped him off then turned to look out the window, his mind whirling. He knew he needed to let CC know about the message, knew he needed to follow up with another report.

And he would. Tonight. When he got home.

Time is drawing near.

He hoped the hell it was, because he was more than ready for this to end.

Chapter Fourteen

According to CC, they had less than an hour to go. Dave certainly hoped so, because he needed to get out and stretch.

He smothered a yawn and glanced around, dividing his attention between the road and the passing scenery. Pine trees. Sandy soil. And lumber trucks. He hadn't expected to see so many down here.

Hell, he hadn't expected to see any down here.

They had made pretty good time heading down I95, even if you counted the traffic around DC and into Virginia. But there was always traffic around there, no matter what time of day it was, so he had been expecting it.

What he hadn't been expecting was the heat and humidity. Not in October. He reached down and adjusted the air conditioning vent so the cold air hit him in the face. But the moist blanket of warm air permeated the inside of the truck, no matter what he did.

He glanced over at CC and shook his head,

helpless to stop his grin. The truck would be a lot cooler if she'd stop lowering the window. She looked over at him, saw him watching her, then shrugged.

"What can I say? I like the smell. Pine trees, fresh air, the water. Not like back in Maryland." She stabbed the control button on the door and the window climbed up, sealing them comfortably in the truck.

And finally letting the cab cool off.

"Is it always this hot down here?"

"It's worse in the summer. But no, it's not usually this bad this time of year. Mom said they were having a heat wave, though, so get used to it." She leaned over and grabbed his phone from the dash, unlocking the screen with a tap and pulling up his text messages. Her brow furrowed as she studied the message he received yesterday, and she mumbled under her breath.

"I still don't like this." She tossed the phone back into the console, staring at it like it might jump up and attack her.

"Yeah, I'm not real crazy about it myself. But what am I supposed to do about it? They can't trace it, have no idea where it's originating from, other than somewhere in Baltimore."

"I just wish there was something else I could do."

"CC, it's not your problem."

"Um, hello? This guy was at my house, remember? That makes it my problem. Besides, I'm not going to let you handle this all on your own."

Dave glanced over at her, saw determination and anger flash in her hazel eyes, and bit back his smile. He shouldn't be smiling. The situation was escalating out of control, if what the police had said was true. He was inclined to agree with them, given the added line to the message.

Time is drawing near.

No, he shouldn't be smiling. But it was nice knowing he had CC on his side.

He reached over and grabbed her hand, giving it a squeeze. "Thank you."

"For what?"

"For just being you."

She squeezed his hand back, but he could see her thinking again. Her eyes narrowed just the tiniest bit as she stared out the window, her lips pursed in deep thought.

"And there's nothing that you can think of that may have started this? You don't remember anyone in particular? No one soldier who stands out?"

Dave breathed in deeply, then exhaled on a sigh. They were treading near dangerous territory, dredging up memories he'd prefer to keep sleeping, bringing up topics he'd prefer not to share.

"CC, there were a lot of soldiers, a lot of patients." He clenched his jaw, exhaled again. "A lot of guys who didn't make it. No, nobody stands out."

And that bothered him more than it should. How many had he patched up? How many times had he tried his best, knowing his best wasn't good enough? Too many times. Too many nameless faces.

Too much death.

She squeezed his hand, hard, then turned in the seat and faced him. "I'm sorry."

"Nothing you can do about it."

"I know. I just wish...well, I just wish you didn't have to worry about this, didn't have to remember."

"It's no different than what I do now." He uttered the lie without thinking, heard her short laugh of disbelief in response. But neither of them said anything else about it, and he knew the subject was closed. For now.

Yet he couldn't help but wonder. Could he have done something more? Was there just one time where, if he had done something differently, there would have been one less Flag-draped coffin? One less grieving family? The life-blood of one less soldier staining the sands in that God forsaken hell hole?

His hand clenched the steering wheel, his knuckles turning white. God, he had to stop thinking that way. Couldn't keep thinking that way, not if he wanted to keep his sanity intact.

My Brother's Keeper.

He had that emblazoned on his chest for a reason. As a reminder. His motto. The motto of so many. A reminder of the responsibility to care for and watch over his brothers-in-arms. And he had to believe he had done his best, had saved as many as he could. It was futile, heartbreaking, unfathomable to think otherwise.

"Make a right coming up here, on 17." CC motioned with her free hand, indicating the road ahead of them. Dave slowed to a stop, checked for traffic, then made the turn. The landscape changed even more, not so many pine trees, the road a little more densely populated.

"You nervous?"

"What?"

"I said, are you nervous? Meeting my family."

Dave glanced over at CC, then turned his attention back to the traffic. He readjusted his grip on the steering wheel, then shrugged. "I wasn't until you just brought it up. Should I be?"

Her clear laughter filled the cab of the truck,

lightening the weight that had been bearing down on his shoulders. Weight and tension he hadn't even realized had been there. He stopped at a traffic light leading into a large shopping center, then turned to look at her.

"Now I'm really worried. Why are you finding this so funny?"

"Sorry. It was just that look on your face, all serious and grumpy again."

"I'm not grumpy."

"I didn't say you were. It was just that expression on your face."

Dave pulled forward with the traffic, his eyes more focused on the road now that traffic was a little heavier. He glanced down at the clock, noticed it was almost four-thirty in the afternoon, and figured they must be in rush hour traffic.

"Don't worry, Mom and Dad will like you. Bubby and Tippy will probably act all Alpha with you but it's just a show, they're harmless."

"Bubby and Tippy? Are they the dogs?"

CC looked over at him, her eyes wide, then started laughing, hard enough that she bent over, holding her stomach. Long minutes went by before she stopped, gasping for air. Dave spared her another glance when they stopped at an intersection, wondering what he said that was so funny.

"Oh, I can't wait to tell them that. That's funny. No, go straight through here." She pointed, indicating the road ahead of them, then wiped her eyes. "Bubby and Tippy, the dogs."

"So. I take it they're not dogs?"

"No, they're my brothers."

Dave turned his head to look at her so quickly, he

actually felt a twinge in his neck. "Your brothers are named Bubby and Tippy?"

"No, silly, those are their nicknames. Bubby is my older brother, Robert. Or Rob, depending on what mood he's in. And Tippy is my younger brother, Tim."

Dave closed his eyes briefly and shook his head, an image of coveralls and banjos coming to mind. "And they got these nicknames how, exactly?"

"Did Angie ever have a nickname for you?"

"Other than pain in the ass? No, why?"

"Well, when I was younger, I had a hard time saying Bobby and Timmy, so I always called them Bubby and Tippy. And the names stuck."

"Remind me to thank Angie when I see her. Pain in the ass is a hell of a lot better than Bubby or Tippy. And thank you, because now, when you introduce them to me, I'm not going to be able to keep a straight face."

CC laughed again then leaned over and jabbed the button for the window, lowering it halfway. Humidity immediately filled the truck, along with a sour odor so pungent, Dave's nose immediately wrinkled in distaste. He glanced left and right, looking for a dead animal or something. CC must have noticed, because she laughed again and pointed to the smoke stacks ahead on their left, just before another bridge.

"That's the paper mill."

"Oh, God. That's what a paper mill smells like? That's, uh. Yeah, that's pretty strong. Holy shit."

"It's usually not quite this strong. Don't worry, you won't notice it as much once we get on the other side of the bridge. And you might want to tone down the language a bit, too. Mom gets upset with too much swearing."

"What swearing?"

"Yeah, you're going to be in trouble. You don't even notice when you do it." She released his hand then reached over and patted his leg, a grin of delight on her face. "Which is good, because maybe she'll leave me alone and get on your case instead. And you don't need to worry about my brothers, at least not tonight." She shifted again in her seat, the third time in less than a minute. Dave glanced over at her and suddenly realized that she was nervous.

And okay, maybe he was, too. He would soon be meeting her parents, her entire family. Wasn't that something usually reserved for serious relationships? And he didn't know what this was they had going on. Friends. More than friends. But a serious relationship?

He hadn't given it much thought and realized now probably wasn't the time for that, anyway.

And yes, he was at least able to admit to himself that he wasn't ready to even think about it.

CC shifted again then pointed. "Second left here. Do me a favor, pull into that gas station real quick after you make the turn."

Dave nodded then hit the gas, the truck shooting forward through a break in traffic. He cut the wheel to make the turn, then pulled into the parking lot and put the truck in park. CC unhooked her seatbelt but instead of getting out of the truck, she leaned across the console, grabbed his shirt, and pulled him toward her. Her mouth closed over his, her tongue teasing his lips before dipping inside his mouth. She tasted like tea and mint and pure desire, and his body reacted instantly.

He dipped his head, leaning closer, and ran his hand through the silken strands of her hair. His palm cupped the back of her head, holding, guiding.

And then she pulled away, her breathing heavy, his body on fire. She leaned in for another quick kiss before he could catch his own breath, then smiled.

"Sorry. I needed my fix just in case we don't get a chance to do that again soon."

Dave cleared his throat, the ramifications of her words finally becoming clear in his muddle brain. Then he groaned.

Of course they wouldn't have a chance to do that again. Or anything else, for that matter. They were going to be at CC's parent's. In their house. Under the same roof. And why was he just now realizing that?

Dave put the truck in gear, then turned back onto the road. Sitting was suddenly uncomfortable, and he tried to shift to ease the slight pain. "About how much longer?"

"Maybe five miles."

Great. Wonderful.

He leaned forward and cranked the air conditioner to high, then aimed the vents down toward his lap.

It was going to be a long week.

Chapter Fifteen

CC grabbed her bag from the back of the truck and tossed it over her shoulder then looked around the yard, not bothering to hide her smile. Pine needles and large brown magnolia leaves covered the centipede grass, winning the never-ending battle her father waged to keep the lawn clear. Mom's crepe myrtles framed the front of the house, their gray bark peeling, the branches spreading out like welcoming arms to greet any guests. CC loved crepe myrtles, had even tried planting some at her own place.

There was a chance one might even survive.

She craned her neck to look around the side of the house, past the trunk of the old live oak, to the pier out back. A grin teased her mouth when she saw the small boat tied up there. If she was lucky, maybe they'd get a chance to take it out, just her and Dave.

Because while she may have secretly grinned at Dave's reaction to that kiss, she hadn't exactly been unaffected by it herself. And she had no illusions that they'd be sharing the same bed.

"Nice house. I didn't realize it was on the water."

"Yeah. That's why I love my place so much. It reminds of home a little. It's a shame it's not summer, though. You should see it when everything's in bloom. All set?" Dave nodded, and CC led the way up the stairs to the front porch, which might as well be the second floor. Dad hadn't taken any chances and built high, just in case of hurricanes. This close to the coast, it made sense to be prepared, just in case. CC knew they had evacuated twice in the last seven years, but there'd only been minimal damage both times. She just hoped it stayed that way.

She pushed through the front door, cool air washing over her, and dropped her bag in the entranceway. "Mom? Dad? We're here!" She glanced over her shoulder at Dave and gave him a reassuring smile, then closed the door and moved down the hallway.

"In here, Carolann."

CC grimaced then shot Dave a dirty look when he chuckled before heading back to the kitchen. Her mom was at the large island, chopping cucumbers and tossing them in a bowl. She put the knife down, wiped her hands on a towel, then looked up.

Her brown eyes immediately widened and she hesitated, her gaze steady on CC. She knew what was coming and shook her head, trying to tell her mom not to say anything, but her mom either didn't notice. Or didn't care.

"Carolann, you're wearing shorts! I don't think I've seen you in shorts in years."

"Mom, it's not a big deal." CC knew she was blushing, could feel the heat spread across her cheeks, and hoped Dave didn't notice. She was afraid to look at him, wondered if he'd think her mom's comment was unusual.

Wondered if he'd realize the meaning behind it.

But she didn't have the chance to do or say anything else, because her mom was suddenly in front of her, hugging her. CC hesitated, then wrapped her own arms around her mother's slender frame and hugged her back. A brief twinge of guilt filled her, because it had been too long between visits. And while her parents weren't old—Dad had just turned sixty-two and Mom was fifty-nine—she knew better than anyone how quickly things could change.

So she relaxed in her mom's embrace, hugging her back, the gentle scent of her favorite floral fragrance tickling her nose and taking her back to her childhood. Then she had to blink, because moisture suddenly filled her eyes and she didn't want anyone to notice.

Her mom pulled away, her hands on CC's shoulders as she gave her a thorough looking over. She must have approved of whatever she saw because she nodded, then turned to Dave.

"And you must be Dave. It's so nice to meet you. I'm Joyce, Carolann's mother." And before Dave could say anything, her mom wrapped him in a hug, too.

CC bit back her grin as Dave looked over at her, his surprise and discomfort clear. He reached out with one big hand and awkwardly patted her mom on the back, then gave her a look that clearly asked for help.

CC laughed just as her mom stepped away, and didn't miss the quick look of relief on Dave's face.

"Nice to meet you, ma'am."

"I'm impressed, Carolann. Not only is he nice to look at, he has manners, too."

"Mom. Really?" Dave shifted behind her, and she

didn't have to turn around to know that his face was probably as red as hers. But her mom just laughed, then waved her hands in a shooing motion at both of them.

"Your dad's out back, getting the grill ready. Why don't you head out there, introduce Dave, and relax before dinner?"

CC didn't waste time, just grabbed Big Guy's hand and dragged him through the kitchen and out the door, to the screened-in porch and out to the lower deck. The door slammed behind them, catching the attention of the man standing over the charcoal grill.

Her dad turned, a smile creasing his weathered face as he stepped forward and wrapped her in a big hug powerful enough to lift her off the floor.

"There's my baby girl!" He finally set her on her feet and gave her a minute to let her catch her breath. His brows went up in brief surprise when he noticed her outfit, but, unlike her mom, at least he didn't say anything. Instead, he turned to Dave with speculation in his dark eyes, one corner of his mouth turned up in a grin.

"You must be Dave. Nice to meet you."

CC paused for the briefest second, wondering how Dave would react at meeting her dad, wondering if she should have given him some warning. To be honest, she hadn't thought about it until just now and she realized she was holding her breath, waiting.

But there was no trace of reaction on Dave's face, not even the barest flinch as he reached out and shook her father's left hand, his grip strong and sure as he ignored the prosthetic arm hanging at her father's right side.

"Mr. Covey, nice meeting you, sir."

"Just call me Ed." He turned back around and

placed the lid on the charcoal grill, then looked over his shoulder. "Why don't you two go get your things settled? Your mother's already set up the front guest room for Dave. Then come on back and we'll have a drink and visit before dinner."

CC rolled her eyes, interpreting her father's words to mean an interrogation. Which she should have expected, since she had never brought anyone home with her before. She just hoped they didn't read too much into it.

No, she corrected, she hoped *she* didn't read too much into it. Yes, Dave had agreed to come down here with her. No, that didn't mean this was a serious relationship, or that it was even headed in that direction. In fact, it meant nothing. Absolutely nothing. She'd do well not to get ahead of herself, to keep her emotions steady, safe. One day at a time.

She led Dave back through the house and up the stairs, pointing out the guest room before moving past him. His hand snaked out and closed around her wrist, pulling her into the room with him. And then his mouth was on hers, hot, greedy. CC leaned into him, her hands fisted in his shirt, liquid desire flowing through her as his tongue plunged into the recesses of her mouth.

A groan escaped her as his hands cupped her ass, squeezing. Then he stepped away, a grin on his face as she tried to catch her breath.

"That's payback for earlier."

"That's cruel. Real cruel, Big Guy." CC backed out of the room, straight into the doorframe before she caught herself. Dave chuckled then winked at her before she hurried down the hall into her own room.

And realized that her emotions had already gotten

way ahead of her.

Chapter Sixteen

Dinner had been a relaxing, informal affair on the screened porch room. Grilled steak, crisp salad, roasted vegetables, fresh rolls. Almost too much food. But Dave had eaten all of it, earning him an approving smile from CC's mother.

The remnants had been cleaned up, the few remaining leftovers put away. Now they were sitting on the lower deck as the night closed over them, taking some of the edge off the heat and humidity. They sat around the low table, watching the water just beyond as citronella-filled tiki torches worked to keep the few bugs away.

Dave leaned back in the comfortable lounge chair, drawing on the cigar CC's father had insisted he have. He had tried to decline, never having really gotten into the cigar fad, but Ed had insisted.

And Dave figured why not. It wasn't like he'd have to worry about CC thinking he tasted like an ashtray later. And the cigar was surprisingly smooth, with just a hint of some mellow spice.

149

It was a nice complement to the smooth bourbon he was drinking.

A click broke the comfortable silence and Dave turned his head, surprised at the grin on CC's face as she snapped his picture with her phone. He raised a brow in her direction but didn't say anything.

"It's not exactly a smile, but I couldn't resist. You look so relaxed, puffing on that cigar, with the drink in your hand."

Dave chuckled and took another puff on the cigar. "Actually, I think I could get used to this."

Ed laughed then raised his own glass in a mock salute before taking a sip. "Nothing wrong with that, son."

Dave raised his own glass in answer, his eyes nonchalantly studying the man seated to his left. He was taller than he had expected, close to six feet, with close cropped dark hair liberally salted with gray. He had the rugged, weathered features of someone who spent a great amount of time outside, and lines on his handsome face that spoke of easy laughter, easy smiles.

CC looked nothing like him.

No, CC was the spitting image of her mother. And if her mother's natural beauty was any indication, CC wouldn't have to worry about aging.

The woman sat next to her husband, a small well-manicured hand resting lightly on his leg. Her light blonde hair was cut into a loose bob that brushed her shoulders, framing an oval face that was just barely showing any signs of age. A few laugh lines around hazel eyes, just the faintest lines near her mouth. Like CC, she was on the shorter side, not as curvy as her daughter. Yes, the mother was attractive.

But the daughter was so much more, with the

looks and personality to make his blood turn hot, to make his senses sing. And thinking like that wasn't going to do him a damn bit of good, not while they were under her parents' roof.

Joyce sipped her wine and turned to face him, her clear look speculative, the hint of a smile on her mouth. "So how did you two meet?"

"Mom, geez, enough already."

"I was just curious. I'm your mother. That's my right."

"We met on a fly-out. At work. Nothing mysterious or over-the-top, okay?" CC shifted in the chair, giving Dave an embarrassed look before hiding her face with her own wine glass.

"Oh, that's right. You did say he was a paramedic. It's nice that you have something in common like that." Joyce's accented voice held a smile, her gaze still speculating as she watched both of them. CC's discomfort was obvious, and Dave realized some of it was rubbing off on him. But her father saved them both from any more potentially embarrassing questions by closing his good hand around his wife's and squeezing.

"Joyce, they just got here. Give them time to relax. You have all week to grill them."

The words weren't what Dave expected, and did nothing to reassure him. CC looked over at him, her eyes reflecting his own thoughts. Then she shrugged, as if to say sorry.

Or maybe it was just her acknowledgement that she could do nothing more than accept her mother's curiosity. Which still didn't do much to reassure him.

Ed drained his glass then stood up, offering his hand to CC's mother. "We're going to go watch some television, I think. You two stay out here and relax, enjoy the night air. Carolann, did you warn Dave about the alligators?"

Dave choked on the swallow of bourbon, his gaze going from Ed to CC and back again. "The what?"

"The gators. They generally stay away, but as a rule, just make sure you turn the light on before you come outside." Ed waved his prosthetic arm around. "You don't want to lose an arm or anything."

"Daddy! I cannot believe you just said that!"

Ed laughed then turned and climbed the steps leading back to the house, Joyce just behind him. Dave watched them leave, his mouth slightly open in shock. He turned back to CC.

"Did he really—"

"No, he didn't. And I have no idea why he said that. He lost his arm in a car accident about sixteen years ago."

"Oh." Dave looked back toward the steps where her parents had disappeared, then took a sip of the bourbon. "So he was just joking about alligators, then?"

"No, he was serious about that."

"Alligators? You really have alligators?"

"Yeah. Not many, and they're not real huge. But they like hanging around the marshy areas, and it's not unusual to see them on the banks sunning themselves. Every once in a while they'll come into the yard, so it's still a good idea to check before you go wandering around. We can go look tomorrow if you want."

Dave watched her for a few long minutes, trying to figure out if she was joking or not. But no, she was serious. He leaned forward and stubbed out what was left of the cigar, then sat back in the chair and stretched his legs out.

"I think I'll pass, thank you."

CC's laughter was soft in the darkness, wrapping around him with a comforting warmth. He reached over and grabbed her hand, threading their fingers together as they sat there, just staring out over the yard.

Yeah, he could get used to this.

And that both surprised and worried him. He'd never been one to think about settling down, never been one to plan his life around what-ifs and maybes, or thinking he needed somebody to share things with. Not that it wasn't for him, just that he had never really given it any thought.

But he was thinking it now, and he wasn't sure if that was a good thing or not. He had no idea what they were doing. Were they really in a serious relationship? Or were they just two people who had met and were merely traveling the same convenient path for right now? It wasn't like they had talked about it, wasn't like they had gone through that whole annoying circling-around-each-other then dating ritual. They had simply met...and now here they were.

And Dave had no idea what to do next. Or even what he wanted to do.

"Uh-oh. Big Guy's deep in thought." CC's teasing voice pulled him back to the here-and-now. She watched him with those clear eyes, and he wondered what she saw when she looked at him. Did she know what he was thinking? Did she think the same thing, or was it nothing more than a fun interlude for her?

He didn't know, and he didn't know how to ask. Worse, part of him was afraid of the answer. He sipped his bourbon, then gave a brief shake of his head.

"Not too deep. Just taking it all in, I guess." Was that disappointment he had seen in her eyes? Or merely wishful thinking?

CC turned away before he could look too closely, the night dark enough that he couldn't clearly read her expression. She lifted the wine glass to her lips and took a small sip, the clear liquid cast in shades of orange from the tiki torches around them. She looked back over at him, her head tilted to the side as she studied him, her teeth gently nibbling on her lower lip. She seemed to be considering something, her expression carefully guarded before she looked away. Her fingers tightened briefly around his as she let out a small sigh.

"He's the reason I still have my leg, you know."

The softly spoken words surprised him, only because he had been expecting something completely different. Dave said nothing for a long minute, just held her hand in his. "Did you want to talk about it?"

She looked over at him and smiled. "That's what's so great about you, Big Guy. You're just, I don't know. There. Laid back and accepting, not judging. If I'm not careful, I could get entirely too accustomed to having you around."

Dave didn't answer, couldn't even if he had known what to say. Her last comment was eerily close to where his own confused thoughts had been leading a few minutes earlier. This was the perfect chance for him to come out and ask, find out from her what she thought they were doing. But he was too worried about what her answer might be, what he would do if it wasn't the answer he had hoped for.

Which was interesting, because he didn't really know what answer he'd want to hear.

But she was watching him, expecting some kind of response, so he latched on to something else she had said instead. "Laid back? I don't think anyone has ever called me that before."

She blinked, her lids covering a brief flare of emotion seen but unrecognized in her eyes, then fixed him with a bright smile. "I beg to differ. You're very calm, very even-keeled."

Dave almost snorted in disbelief, but she shook her head, her expression serious now. "No, you are. I'm not saying you're like that all the time, but from what I've seen so far, you're pretty steady. That's a good thing, so stop complaining."

"Okay, no more complaining." He sipped at the bourbon, his gaze focused straight ahead, waiting. Wondering if she'd explain her comment about her leg, or if her tangent had been a way to deflect attention from something she regretted saying.

Night sounds surrounded them. The chirping of crickets, a hoot of an owl somewhere in the distance. The gentle lapping of waves against the shoreline fifty yards away. Dave rested his head against the back of the chair and closed his eyes, feeling the intimacy of the night settle around them. His thumb stroked CC's hand in gentle circles, her skin soft and smooth beneath his.

"That was an option, you know. Amputation." CC's voice was just above a whisper, filled with reluctance, hesitation. Dave didn't open his eyes, didn't move except for the gentle squeeze of his hand on hers. She would tell him, or she wouldn't. If she chose to, it would be on her terms, in her own way. Silent minutes stretched around them and Dave thought that maybe she had changed her mind. Or maybe she had already said everything she could say.

Dave heard the quiet sound of her sipping, knew she was drinking the last of her wine. "I wanted them to. I thought if they'd just take the damn thing off, the pain would stop. I wasn't afraid to lose it, because I knew what to expect from watching Dad. I didn't think it'd be a big deal, you know? Anything to get rid of the pain."

She paused, clearing her throat. Dave squeezed her hand in silent encouragement, waiting for her to continue. Wondering if she'd continue.

She finally laughed, a short humorless sound filled with self-recrimination. "Dad was furious. I don't think I've ever seen him that mad before. And not at the doctor. He was furious with me. A few of those weeks are still a little fuzzy, but I remember that. I was at Walter Reed, and Dad came flying into the room, yelling. I mean, yelling so loud that they almost escorted him out. And then he let me have it. He, uh..." Her voice drifted off and she cleared it again. Dave opened his eyes and glanced over at her, the flames of the torches reflecting in her bright eyes. She tilted the empty glass against her mouth then looked down at it, frowning. Dave handed her the glass of bourbon and she took it with a small smile of thanks then sipped.

"What happened?"

"He, uh." She cleared her throat and took another sip. "Well, he called me a coward, and said he didn't raise his daughter to be a quitter. And I couldn't understand why he was so upset and told him it wasn't a big deal, that he made out just fine without his arm. That just made it worse."

She stared into the glass, her moist eyes distant and faraway, and Dave knew she was reliving those moments. That they were as clear to her now as if they were just happening. "He told me that he didn't have a choice when he lost his arm, but I did. I tried to explain to him how much pain I was in, but he was having none of it. Just kept telling me how much I had to lose, telling me all the things I'd never be able to do if I let them take it. And not because I wouldn't have a leg, but because I was a quitter, taking the easy way out. If I didn't have the courage to fight through the pain, then I wouldn't have the courage to do everything else."

CC took a deep breath followed by another swallow of bourbon. She put the glass on the table, then angrily brushed at her eyes with the heel of her hand. "And then...then he made me choose."

Dave swallowed against the tightness in his throat, squeezing her hand once more in encouragement, in support. "Choose?"

"Yeah." Another humorless laugh escaped her. "If I wanted to be a coward and let them take the leg, he wouldn't stop me. But I'd lose him too."

"Guess he figured that might help with your decision, huh?"

CC looked over at him, her eyes slowly focusing on him instead of the past. One corner of her mouth lifted in a sad smile as she shook her head. "Yeah, but not at first. I really didn't think I could handle the pain. But Dad is nothing if not stubborn, and he knows me too well. Being called a coward, by my own father, finally sunk in. So yeah, I made my choice. There wasn't a day that went by that I wasn't cussing him up one side and down the other. But he was there, each day, him and mom both until I was finally allowed to leave. And here I am."

Dave offered her a smile then tugged on her hand, pulling until she got up from her chair and sat across his lap. She tucked her head on his shoulder and he dropped a kiss on her head. He wrapped his arms around her, holding her close, holding her just a little too tightly.

"And here you are. Do you regret it?"

"No. No, of course not. And I don't resent him either." Her voice was relaxed now, more like her normal self now that she was no longer reliving the past. Now that the memories were simply that: memories. "It wasn't easy, not at first. And I had to go through all sorts of hurdles to get my job back. But it all worked out."

"Then I'm glad your dad fought for you. You know that's what he was doing, right?"

"Yeah, I know." She tilted her face up, her gaze catching his, holding it. She reached out and traced his lips with her fingers, and he could feel the slight trembling in their gentle touch. He lowered his head and pressed his mouth to hers, the kiss sweet, gentle, reassuring. Lingering.

He ran his hand down her side, past her hips and along her leg, further to the soft skin beneath the hem of her shorts. Lower, to the ropy scars that covered her calf. His touch was gentle, reassuring, as he lifted his mouth from hers.

"For what it's worth, I'm glad he fought for you, too. Not because of your leg, but because I may not have met you otherwise." His whisper was as quiet as the night, meant for her ears only before drifting away into the torch-lit shadows surrounding them. CC's answering smile was bright, lighting her eyes with a glow.

"Mom and Dad are going to think you're something pretty special."

"Yeah? Why is that?"

"Because even though I accepted it, I've never

been very big on others seeing it, including them. My leg, I mean. Except for when I was in physical therapy, I think this is the first time they've seen me in anything but long pants."

Dave pulled back, surprised at her words. He hadn't expected to hear her hesitant admission and didn't know what to make of it. "Really? I would have never thought that of you. Why not?"

"You get enough stares and questions, you tend to get a little self-conscious. I told you, it freaks most people out."

"Well, most people are assholes."

"And that right there is why they're going to think you're something special."

He looked down at her, his eyes searching hers, not knowing what he was looking for. Not knowing what he was seeing. And he wanted to ask if she thought the same, realized he wanted to know the answer to that question. But then she leaned up and kissed him, and the only thing he could think of was how good she felt in his arms, and how much he wanted her.

Chapter Seventeen

The bite of tangy salt air. The sweet smell of coconut-laced lotion. A heavy breeze that whipped the waves with white foam.

Up. Down. Up. Up. Down.

Dave grabbed the railing and closed his eyes as the large boat cut through the waves, putting the coast further behind them. Closing his eyes didn't help. In fact, it made the rolling in his stomach worse as the bourbon and cigar from last night mixed into an unwelcome sour concoction with each rise and dip.

A hand closed over his arm, dry against the clamminess of his skin. He cracked one eye open and glanced down at the hand, but couldn't make the effort to look over at its owner.

Not that it made any difference. He knew it was CC, coming to check on him.

"You okay, Big Guy? You're looking a little green."

Dave swallowed and managed a nod. He may have even mumbled something but he couldn't be sure. His entire focus was on keeping the contents of his stomach in place.

"Why didn't you tell me you get seasick? I could have made some excuse not to go."

"I didn't think I did." He accepted the bottle of water she held out to him, torn between drinking it or pouring it over his head. He opted for drinking it and took a cautious sip.

"Here, try this." He looked down at her hand to see what looked like two pieces of wrapped candy. "They're ginger chews. They might help."

Dave unwrapped them and quickly popped them in his mouth, the sharp taste of ginger exploding on his tongue. He took another sip of water then looked over at the three men standing in the wheel house of the boat.

Ed. Bubby. Tippy.

Hell of a way to make an impression on her family.

He turned back to the railing and closed his eyes, swallowing. Hard. Yeah, the only way he could make an even better impression would be to hang his head over the side and empty the contents of his stomach into the rolling waves around them.

His hands tightened on the railing, turning his knuckles white, and he clenched his jaw. He was not going to toss his cookies. He just wasn't.

"It'll get better once we get out there."

Dave nodded but didn't say anything. As bad as he felt, he could still hear the slight doubt in CC's quiet voice, and he wondered if she was trying to convince him—or herself.

This fishing trip had been her mother's idea. A chance for the boys to bond, as she had put it. And CC had joined them, no questions asked. Almost like she was afraid to leave the four of them alone.

Her father, the former Marine.

Bubby, the FBI agent.

Tippy, the Charleston PD cop.

And him. The seasick, green-gilled paramedic.

When Joyce had first mentioned it, he thought they were taking the small boat he had noticed docked at the pier. That the four of them would go out and play in the calm waters. Toss their lines in the water and just kick back and relax for a leisurely day. It wasn't until this morning, before the crack of dawn, that he learned otherwise.

And he had no idea why he thought this was going to be a fun excursion when they left the house over two hours ago. Her brothers had shown up bright and early, just in time for breakfast and introductions. Then they had loaded up in two trucks, stopped at a store to buy snacks and drinks and sunscreen, and headed toward a marina in Pawley's Island.

Somehow Dave had ended up in the truck with her two brothers, both of whom were miniature versions of her father. Only not so miniature because they were closer to Dave's height and build.

They had been casual in their questions, even joking and laughing during the interrogation. And Dave didn't think for one minute that it was anything less than just that.

How did you meet? At work.

How long have you been seeing each other? A couple of months. And yeah, he knew that was a stretch, but figured it was technically true, sort of, since they had met each other the beginning of September and it was now October.

How serious are you? He had deflected that one,

telling them they needed to talk to CC if they wanted an answer.

They had been like three alpha dogs, scratching, sniffing, clawing for top spot, and Dave still wasn't sure who had won. The irony wasn't lost on him and he knew he owed Angie yet another apology.

Now if only he could get his stomach to settle down.

"I think you made an impression on them."

Dave grunted, then looked over his shoulder again. "Yeah. It'll be an even better one if I hurl."

CC laughed and ducked under his arm until he released his death grip on the railing. He draped his arm over her shoulder, taking some comfort in having her close.

"Don't worry, they like you. So how'd the interrogation go?"

He grunted again. "Remind me to apologize to Angie when we get home."

CC laughed, the sound floating in the wind around them before being carried away. "Sucks being on the other end of all that brotherly protection, huh?"

He didn't answer because he didn't need to. CC had summed it up perfectly in her usual eloquent way.

He closed his eyes and took another deep breath of salty air and sunscreen. Was it his imagination, or had his stomach settled just a bit already? At this point, he didn't care. As long as his body stopped threatening to turn traitor on him, he'd take it.

Thirty minutes and an additional two ginger chews later, he was almost back to normal. It helped that they were stopped now, the waves no longer quite as intimidating. The conversation was light-hearted and casual as they assembled rods, reels and lines, the slightly rotten smell of herring and squid filling the air. Dave briefly closed his eyes against the slight churning in his stomach, then opened them again at the chuckle coming from behind.

"Keep it down, Big Guy. I don't feel like losing my bet."

Dave turned to see Rob grinning at him with a crooked smile that almost looked out of place on the rugged planes of his face.

"Bet?"

"Yeah. I got twenty riding against you hurling. Tim still thinks he has a chance to win. Don't spoil it for me."

"Great. I'll do my best, trust me." Dave ignored the chuckle and looked down at the rod in his hand, not quite sure what to do with it. He had been fishing before, but never deep sea fishing, and he was waiting to see what everyone else did before he made an even bigger ass of himself.

He looked around, searching for CC, and saw her standing near the stern, slathering more sunscreen on her legs and arms. She must have sensed him watching her because she glanced over her shoulder and smiled, a slow seductive smile that dried his mouth. She grabbed the hem of her tank shirt and pulled it over her head, revealing a bright green bikini top that matched the colorful board shorts she was wearing. The top wasn't revealing, was actually modest, but it still allowed him a glimpse of her full breasts and generous cleavage. She winked at him then stepped onto the transom and dove into the water.

"Dammit CC!" Rob and Tim shouted in unison while her father mumbled under his breath. Dave looked at all three, wondering at their sudden scramble as they moved to the stern, watching.

"That damn girl is going to kill herself one of these days."

"I swear to God, she has a death wish."

Dave moved closer, sudden unexplained worry clenching his gut as he searched the water, waiting for CC to surface. "What is it? What's wrong?"

"What's wrong is that my sister thinks she has to keep proving herself, and it's going to kill her one of these days." Rob spoke between clenched teeth, his gaze intent as he scanned the water.

"But she's a strong swimmer, she does it all the time."

"Yeah, but cold water cramps her calf. I don't give a shit how strong a swimmer she is, she gets a leg cramp and it won't be good."

"And the water isn't exactly warm."

Dave gulped down the sudden concern seizing him as he kept watching, waiting for CC to surface. Tense silence gripped the four of them, but none of the other three men seemed ready to jump overboard in a rescue attempt.

So maybe Dave was just overreacting.

CC's head broke the surface more than ten yards away. She whipped the hair from her face then waved at them with a broad smile.

"Carolann Marie Covey, you get back to this boat right now." Ed bellowed the command in a voice not be argued with, his finger pointed in her direction in parental demand.

"I just wanted to cool off."

"No, you wanted to show off. Now get back here, you're scaring the fish." Tim shook his head then turned away from the stern, moving to get his rod from where it leaned against the side. Rob and Ed watched her for a few seconds before they, too, moved away. Rob paused next to him, a frown on his face.

"Keep an eye on her, make sure she actually listens for once."

Dave merely nodded then looked back over the water, watching CC as she bobbed in the waves, her strong strokes pulling her through the water toward them. He opened the transom door and stepped out onto the platform, kicking the swim ladder down. Cold water splashed over his feet, chilling him. He ignored the sensation, waiting, watching, as she swam closer.

She stopped about ten feet away, smiling up at him as she tread water in the waves. "Hey Big Guy. Care to join me?"

"No, I'll pass. It's a little too cold for me. C'mon, get back up here."

"Don't be a chicken. Remember how much fun we had the last time we went swimming?"

Instant heat erupted inside him, going to straight to his groin. Remember? How could he forget? He still relived that night—and every night they had been together since—in his mind. He felt his face turn red and he glanced behind him, wondering if her father or brothers had heard her, wondering if they would be able to see the guilt written all over his face.

But they didn't seem to be paying attention, more focused on the fishing gear surrounding them. He turned back to CC, noticed that she was laughing as she looked up at him.

"Are you blushing?"

"No idea what you're talking about."

"Yeah, you do. Your face is all red."

"That's sunburn."

CC's grin clearly told him that she knew better but she didn't say anything. She kicked her legs behind her, her strong arms pulling her closer to the boat as the waves fought to keep her back. She closed the distance by several feet then stopped, a grimace suddenly contorting her face. Dave watched as she took a deep breath and let it out, her hands disappearing under the surface. He straightened, nerves taut, on edge.

"CC?"

"I'm good." She took another deep breath before her head disappeared below the surface for a frightening second. She came back up, her right arm flailing against a wave as she was pulled a little further from the boat.

Another grimace twisted the delicate features of her face. She looked at him, tried to smile as another wave tugged at her.

"Shit." Dave pushed off the swim platform, his body slicing through the cold water, salt stinging his eyes as he kicked his way under the waves. He surfaced just in front of CC and reached out, grabbing her.

"I'm fine, it's just a cramp."

He didn't say anything, just held on to her and swam toward to the boat, his free arm pulling with strong strokes, his powerful legs kicking behind them. Three concerned faces looked down at them, hands outstretched to help them back in. They were almost to the boat, Dave ready to push CC in front of him so Rob could help her out, when her hands tightened around his arm, her nails digging into his flesh.

Dave looked down, his pulse rate off the charts, afraid that something else was wrong, something more than just a cramp.

As if that wasn't bad enough.

But CC's eyes were clear of fear and anxiety, filled with something different. Determination. Stubbornness. Pride.

"Don't tell them what happened." Her whispered plea barely reached his ears, nearly lost in the cold water lapping around them. Then she pushed away from him, breaking his hold on her, and swam the last few feet with awkward strokes.

Dave watched as two sets of hands reached for her, pulling her up as she tried to brush them off and climb the ladder on her own. He could tell she wasn't putting any weight on her left leg, could tell that it was still cramping.

Did she honestly think nobody else would notice?

He clenched his jaw, his concern morphing into misplaced anger, and climbed up after her. She was standing at the stern, a strained smile on her face, doing her best to convince everyone that she was fine, that Dave had overreacted, that there had been no need for him to jump in after her.

CC was so convincing that even he almost fell for it and he started to wonder if maybe he really had overreacted. Then his gaze locked on hers for a brief second and he realized it was all a sham, a show put on for the benefit of her father and brothers.

He turned away and reached for a towel, drying himself off. Trying to brush away the irrational anger that gripped him, trying to figure out where the anger was coming from.

And trying his damnedest not to admit that she had scared the living hell out of him.

Chapter Eighteen

The waves had gentled even more, creating a soothing rocking beneath the hull of the boat, a comforting sensation that tried to lull CC into sleep. Actually, she was pretty sure she *had* drifted off, if only for a few minutes.

She opened her eyes, squinting into the sun, then rolled onto her stomach and grabbed the novel she had been reading. The sun was warm and prickly against her skin, long since dried from her impromptu swim a few hours ago.

Dave was mad at her. In fact, every infuriating, testosterone-poisoned male of the species on this boat was mad at her. Except for maybe the fish they had been catching. No, the scaly creatures were probably mad at her, too.

And the anger was misplaced. Granted, it was probably more irritation than anger on the part of her dad and her brothers. But not Dave. And she didn't understand why.

They had all overreacted. Dave by jumping in after

her, everyone else by getting mad because she had needed help. At least, that's what they thought.

But she hadn't needed help. She would have been fine. Yes, she got a leg cramp. So what. She hadn't panicked, was taking her time rubbing it, smoothing it out with her hands. Yeah, she had drifted a little further away from the boat. It wasn't a big deal, she would have made the swim back with no problem once she dealt with the cramp.

But Dave had decided to jump in after her, which made everyone else stop what they were doing to come watch.

To come help.

And she hadn't needed the help, but she couldn't convince any of them of that.

Testosterone poisoning. Plain and simple.

She peered over the top of the book and looked toward the rear of the boat. All four of them were lounging around, drinks in hand as their rods sat unwatched in the holders, lines lax as they bobbed somewhere in the depths below them. Conversation and laughter drifted toward her and she ground her teeth in irritation. Just like her mom had hoped, they were all bonding, joking around and having a good old time.

And apparently talking about her, because she could catch her name every once in a while.

They were frustrating. All four of them. And to think she had come on this trip so Dave wouldn't feel threatened or outnumbered. So he wouldn't worry about her brothers trying to throw him overboard in the middle of the ocean.

He'd be lucky if *she* didn't throw him overboard. The traitor.

"Carolann, are you going to stay up there and pout all day, or are you going to come down here and have lunch?" Her dad's booming voice floated back to her and she narrowed her eyes, just because.

"I'm not pouting."

"Let her go hungry, Dad. More for us."

"Yeah, let her stay up there and get fried, that'll teach her."

"I'm not getting fried. I have sunscreen on."

Male laughter filled the air and she gritted her teeth again. Maybe she could throw all four of them overboard and be done with it. Except her mom would probably get upset with her if she did that.

Then again, maybe not. Surely her mom, of all people, would understand.

She ignored the laughter and conversation and turned her attention back to the book, trying to lose herself in the words on the page. A shadow fell across her, pulling her attention from the dashing pirate hero, and she looked up in irritation, pushing her sunglasses on top of her head.

And realized that Dave looked exactly as she had pictured the pirate hero to look. Tall, broad, dark hair and piercing eyes. The dark shadow of a two-day beard covered his square jaw, making him look wild and untamed. Much like the pirate in the book.

But instead of wearing an open, billowing linen shirt, her pirate had on an unbuttoned fishing shirt and bathing trunks that hung low on his trim hips. Instead of tall black boots, her pirate was barefooted. And instead of wielding a wicked cutlass, her pirate was carrying a plate of food and two bottles of beer.

She liked her pirate better, even if he was wearing the same dangerous, brooding expression as the book pirate.

She lowered her sunglasses then turned back to the book. "You are blocking my sun."

Dave ignored her and lowered himself to the deck beside her, without dropping anything, which impressed her. But she didn't say anything and pretended to keep reading. "I brought you lunch."

He put the plate between them then held out one of the beers, pushing it close enough to her face that she could feel the coolness of the bottle through the air. She took a deep breath and let it out in a heavy sigh meant to tell him she wasn't impressed with the peace offering. But she reached out and took the bottle anyway, turning on her side so she could take a sip.

She couldn't see Dave's eyes through the dark lenses of his glasses, but knew his gaze dropped to her chest. She could feel the heat of his eyes against her skin, just the look enough to pucker her nipples. He swallowed and looked away, shifting against the hard fiberglass deck.

"Why are you pouting?"

"I am not pouting. I am a grown woman. Grown women do not pout." The corner of his mouth turned up in a small grin then disappeared. At least he was smart enough not to respond, which made her smile.

"Then why are you up here by yourself?"

"Why are you mad at me?"

"I never said I was mad at you."

She raised one eyebrow in disbelief and reached for some of the chips on the plate. "Really? Is that why you've been glaring at me for the last few hours?"

"I have not been glaring."

"Okay, glowering then."

"I haven't been glowering." He lowered his glasses

and narrowed his eyes at her, making her laugh.

"Then what do you call that?"

"Staring at you. In confusion."

She threw a chip at him then took a sip of beer, done with the banter for now. "Why did you jump in after me?"

"Because I thought you needed help."

"I didn't. I would have been fine."

"I didn't know that, did I? What the hell did you want me to do? Wait until you were actually drowning? What the hell, CC." He pushed his sunglasses back up his face then ran a hand through his hair. Frustration poured from him in waves, thick in the air around them. A muscle jumped in his clenched jaw as he turned and looked out over the water, his chest rising and falling with deep measured breaths.

CC sighed and looked down at the bottle in her hand. "I really was fine, you know."

"Fine. You were fine. Excuse me for thinking you needed help. Excuse me for having the living fuck scared out of me." He hissed the words through clenched teeth and CC knew, without a doubt, that he wanted to shout them instead. Then the meaning of the words finally sunk in and she felt a second's surprise when she realized he really had been worried. Not just concerned, but actually worried. How'd he put it? He had the living fuck scared out of him.

She tried not to smile, knew it was a completely irrational reaction and that it would probably only upset him more if he saw it. So she hid the smile by taking another swallow of beer, then reached out and closed her hand around his thigh. "Thank you. For being worried."

"Don't thank me. Next time I'll just let your ass

drown."

CC bit the inside of her cheek, wanting to ask him who was pouting now but thinking better of it. She slid her hand a little higher on his thigh, her fingers tracing lazy circles against his skin. He stiffened under her touch, his hand closing around her wrist.

"What are you doing?"

"Nothing." She wiggled her fingers and he loosened his grip on her wrist. She slid her hand up further, inside the leg of his swimming trunks, teasing the sensitive skin high on the inside of his thigh.

He inhaled quickly and grabbed her hand, moving it so her palm was flat against the deck. Then he leaned on it so she couldn't move it. "Are you trying to get me thrown overboard?"

"No."

"Then stop."

She tried moving her hand but Dave wouldn't budge. "I can't eat with you leaning on my hand."

"I thought you said you weren't hungry."

"I am now." She tried pulling her hand free, then sighed in mock surrender. "I'll behave. Honest."

Dave watched her, disbelief clear on his face, then muttered something under his breath before releasing her hand. She grinned then sat up, her smile teasing as she reached for the plate.

"We could stage a mutiny, you know."

"A mutiny?"

"Yeah. We could throw all three of them overboard, then you could ravage me belowdecks."

"Ravage you?"

"Yeah. You know, tie me up, have your way with me."

Dave groaned, an almost breathless sound of

frustration as he glanced over his shoulder, making sure nobody else was listening. He shifted then looked down at her, his expression unreadable. "You said you'd behave."

"I am behaving! See, I'm keeping my hands to myself!" She held up both hands as proof.

"That's not behaving."

"Hmm. Maybe you need to punish me."

Dave ran one hand down his face and shifted again, saying something that sounded suspiciously like swearing. CC laughed and sipped her beer, letting her gaze wander along his body.

"Or I could ravage you. Tie you down spread eagle, kiss every inch of your body, straddle your big—"

"Okay, I'm done. No more." He jumped to his feet and adjusted himself with a frown, then looked down at her. "Just remember, payback. When you least expect it, I will get you back."

"Is that a promise, Big Guy?"

He groaned again and walked away, leaving her alone with her lunch and laughter. She had never teased anyone that way before and enjoyed it more than she should have.

Even if it did leave her just as frustrated as it left him.

Chapter Nineteen

Flames burned low in the stone fire pit, tossing a ring of amber light and flickering shadows around the circle. Conversation ran in bits and spurts, quiet and relaxed, the breaks in-between filled with the sounds of night.

Dave puffed on the cigar and followed it with a sip of bourbon, thinking he could get used to this nightly routine. The only thing that would make it better was having CC in his bed at the end of it.

His body tightened at the mere thought of it and he realized, not for the first time, that the past three days had been the most sexually frustrated he had been in a long time. Three days. It shouldn't have been a problem at all, not considering he had gone longer—much longer—in the past. But she was always there, smiling at him, teasing him, with a word or a glance or a gesture. Like yesterday afternoon on the boat, when he had been tempted to dive into the chilly waves to control his reaction.

She was driving him crazy, and there was nothing

he could do about it.

Not while they were staying at her parents' house. Not with her brothers here.

He didn't think they were actually watching his every move, but he knew all too well how protective brothers could be. Guilt surged through him each time he thought of what he wanted to do CC, and he caught himself more than once looking over his shoulder, wondering if his thoughts showed on his face. Then waiting to see if either of her brothers noticed, wondering if he was about to make facial contact with four fists.

He looked over at the brothers now, both of them sprawled in the camp chairs, their poses eerily similar to his. One dark, one light, their individual coloring coming from each parent. But both of them had their father's build: tall, strong, sturdy. Dave was good at reading people and knew without a doubt that neither of them would hesitate to get physical in defense of their sister—or anything else, if it came right down to it. It was both comforting and disconcerting knowing that he had so much in common with them.

"When you guys heading back?"

"Friday morning, from what CC tells me."

Rob shared a knowing look with his brother, then both men chuckled. Dave frowned, looking from one to the other, not understanding the joke. Tim raised his glass toward Dave, a grin on his face.

"She's got you all tied up in knots, doesn't she?"

"Who? CC? No, why?"

"'From what CC tells me'?" Tim threw his words back at him, the grin still in place. "Sounds like she's calling the shots."

Dave shifted in the chair, feeling defensive, like he

had to explain things for some reason. "No, she's not calling the shots. This is her trip, I'm just along for the ride. As long as I'm back at work on Sunday morning, I don't care what we do."

Rob shook his head, his dark eyes sparkling with laughter. "Don't deny it, man. Baby sister has you spinning in all sorts of directions."

Dave opened his mouth to deny it, then figured it was safer not to say anything so he just took another draw on the cigar. Yes, she did have him spinning. Just look at how frustrated she had gotten him over the last three days. He had never met anyone else who could do that to him and he wasn't sure what to make of it.

"We're not teasing you. Much. It's just nice to realize her influence reaches past family. She's had us wrapped around her finger ever since she was born."

"Speak for yourself, big brother. I was the one she tormented growing up. That girl was a pain in my ass. Still is."

"You're just mad that she used to beat the living crap out of you."

Dave laughed and looked over at Tim, surprised to see the big man squirming in his chair. Was his face red from embarrassment, or was it just a reflection of the fire? He couldn't tell, thought maybe it was a bit of both. Tim ran his hand through his hair, causing the blonde strands to stick up in various directions and giving him a disheveled appearance. An image of a shorter, petite CC jumping on a younger Tim and tormenting him formed in his mind, as clear as if he was seeing it unfold in front of him. He laughed again and raised his glass toward the big man.

"Poor Tippy. I can imagine it must have been mortifying."

Tim's mouth dropped open as Rob's bark of laughter echoed around them, startling whatever wildlife was nearby into silence.

"I'm going to kill her!"

"Sounds like your secret is out now. Tippy." Rob laughed again, and Dave turned to him, a smile on his face.

"Yeah, it is. Bubby."

Their reactions instantly switched, with Tim now laughing and surprised irritation clear on Rob's face. He swallowed a healthy slug of bourbon then shook his head. "Damn her. I didn't think she'd actually tell anyone about those stupid names. When the hell did she tell you that?"

"On the way down here. She told me that you both would probably sniff me over, but that you were harmless and I shouldn't worry about it." Dave looked at each man then grinned. "I thought she was talking about the dogs."

"Dogs. Great."

"I think we're going to have a little chat with Miss Carolann later tonight."

The three men looked each other then laughed, some silent admission passing around them that CC had somehow gotten the better of all three of them. Rob leaned back in the chair and stretched his legs in front of him, staring into the fire for a few minutes. He took several puffs on the cigar, then looked over at Dave, his gaze speculative, searching.

"So what else has CC told you?"

Dave heard what lay underneath the question and felt a second's discomfort. He met the man's gaze straight on. "About?"

"You've obviously seen her leg. What'd she tell

you about it?"

Dave finally looked away from the man's piercing gaze and took a long swallow from his nearly-empty glass. Was Rob looking for details? Or did he just want to know how much Dave knew? "Enough. Everything."

"Everything? Like what?"

Dave looked up, saw both men watching him carefully. He took a deep breath and let it out slowly, then answered in a quiet voice. "About the ambush. The soldier she was trying to protect. How she almost opted for amputation."

Stunned silence greeted his words, stretching tight around them. He saw the two brothers exchange a long look, one filled with wordless communication before they both turned and looked at him.

"Get the fuck out. No shit."

"She's never told either one of us what happened. Never. I can't believe she told you." Rob pinned him with an intense look, his dark eyes serious, assessing, gauging. Dave didn't look away, didn't move, didn't do anything but meet that questioning stare straight on. But inside he was squirming, discomfort making him edgy as he wondered if he had just betrayed a confidence he hadn't realized he'd been privy to.

"Dad knew. At least part of it, which is how we knew. I'm thinking that maybe even he doesn't know all of it."

Or maybe he did, and hadn't felt the need to share, which is what Dave had just done. He wanted to sink into the ground, or throw himself into the fire. Instead, he leaned forward and crushed what was left of the cigar in the ashtray, wondering again how much of CC's confidence in him he had just betrayed.

Tim reached over and patted him on the shoulder. "Hey man, don't sweat it. We're not going to tell her you said anything, don't worry."

"You won't, but I will. I didn't realize you hadn't known, or I wouldn't have said anything at all."

The brothers exchanged another look of wordless communication then turned back to him. Something had changed in that brief moment, something that made him sit back, slightly stunned. After the initial interrogation yesterday, the three of them had been cordial, friendly. It was a new acquaintance that may or may not evolve into friendship based on his relationship with CC. In other words, they were nice to him because he was dating their sister.

But now there was something else. He saw respect and admiration in their gazes. Acceptance, not for who he was to their sister, but for who he was, period. He wasn't sure what to make of it, wasn't sure how he should take it.

The moment of realization passed in the blink of an eye, leaving them cloaked in camaraderie that went beyond their recent acquaintance. Dave stretched out in the chair, feeling more relaxed than he had just an hour ago—a feeling no doubt aided by the refill of bourbon Tim had poured into his glass.

The conversation drifted to more mundane topics, including their upcoming trip to Charleston in the morning. Something both brothers found amusing, considering that CC generally didn't bother making the hour drive to the charming city. Tim gave him some advice on what to see, and what to stay away from him. Then he laughed and warned Dave about CC's obsession with sweetgrass baskets.

"I'll bet you right now, she dumps at least three

hundred dollars tomorrow."

Dave sputtered and choked, then looked over at Tim. "Three hundred dollars? On a basket? On *one* basket?"

"As much as it pains me to defend her, it's money well spent. These things can take weeks to make, and they're all done by hand." Rob's explanation did nothing to alleviate Dave's surprise.

"Yeah, it's almost a dying art. And they are kind of cool. If you're into that sort of thing. Mom has some in the kitchen and dining room if you want to take a look."

"No thanks. I can't exactly see me buying a basket for that kind of money, I don't care what it looks like."

Rob laughed and exchanged another glance with Tim. "You will. Especially if CC drags you to the Market. She'll walk you from one end to the other and ooh and ahh over all the vendors until she finds something she likes. Then you'll stand there for fifteen minutes, watching the ladies weave their magic. CC will fork over money for one she wants, then you'll start thinking that maybe you should go ahead and get one. Just a small one, as a little souvenir of your time in Charleston."

"Yeah, until you come back down and then decide to get another one."

Dave shook his head again in denial. "Not happening, I don't care what you say."

"What's not happening?"

Dave turned at the sound of CC's voice, a grin tugging at the corner of his mouth when she stopped behind him and leaned over the back of his chair. She slid her arms around him, letting them rest against his chest as she pressed her mouth against his, her lips warm and soft. He groaned when she teased his tongue with hers, groaned again when she pulled away.

Then she grabbed the glass from his hand and straightened, taking a healthy sip. "So what's not happening?"

"Bubby and Tippy here are convinced I'm going to be spending money on baskets tomorrow when we go to Charleston."

CC choked on the bourbon, looked at Dave in surprise, then turned to her brothers. "Oops."

"Yeah, oops. You are so busted."

CC rolled her eyes then looked back at Dave, who chuckled at her total lack of remorse. "And you will."

"I will what?"

"Buy a basket. Trust me, everyone does. Even those two over there, acting all innocent."

"Is that a fact?" Dave turned back and noticed Rob and Tim both were glaring at their sister.

"Christ CC, is nothing a secret with you?" Tim shook his head in mock disgust. But CC didn't seem to mind, just stuck her tongue out at him before grabbing Dave's hand and pulling him from the chair.

"Mom said to bring the glasses inside when you're done, and to put the fire out before you come in. And Dad said there better be something left in that bottle, or you're both buying him one. Each."

Tim reached for the bottle at his feet, lifting it up into the firelight. Less than an inch of amber liquid floated in the bottom. "Oops."

"It was his fault." Rob pointed at Dave with a glass that was half-filled, then immediately lowered the evidence. CC just shook her head then started tugging on Dave's hand, leading him back toward the house.

"Where are you going?"

"Mom and Dad are watching the news, and I'm going to bed."

"You have to drag Dave with you?"

"Yes, I do."

"Why?"

CC paused and turned back to her brothers, her face scrunched in a perfect expression of sibling frustration. "Really?"

Rob punched Tim in the shoulder, then raised his glass toward both of them. "She thinks she's going to get a chance for some alone time, you dip shit. Like Mom and Dad aren't smart enough to figure that out."

"Watch it, Bubby. Remember, I know all the secrets and I'm not afraid to spill them." She turned back around, ignoring the laughter that followed them to the house.

Dave knew exactly what she was doing, because it had become a ritual the last two nights. They went into the house to say goodnight to her parents while they watched the news, then continued upstairs.

To get ready for bed.

Dave pulled her into the guest room and immediately into his arms, their mouths coming together in a frenzy, their hands hurried, desperate. The quick make-out sessions—he had no idea what else to call them—made him feel like a hormone-crazed teenager, hungering for a chance to reach third base.

Except this hunger was edgier than any he had felt as a teen, sharp with the knowledge of what it was like to be with the woman in his arms. His hands cupped around her ass and pulled her closer, his erection throbbing against the soft curves of her body. He pulled his mouth from hers, his breathing ragged, desperate.

"You're driving me crazy. I don't think I can keep this up much longer."

Her hand dipped between them, her palm rubbing against his hard length as she gave him a wicked smile. "Hmm, I think you can keep it up for quite a long time."

He groaned, pressing himself against her hand, then forced himself to push her away. She looked up at him, the question clear in her eyes as he ran a hand through his hair and over his face.

"CC. I..." He paused, not knowing how to say what he needed to say, then decided to just come right out and say it. "I think I screwed up with your brothers."

"You seriously want to talk about them right now?"

"No. This isn't about them."

"Then what is it?"

"When we were talking. They, uh, they asked if I knew about your leg, wanted to know how much I knew."

"They did, did they? Why am I not surprised?"

"No, you don't understand. When they asked, I told them you had told me everything. The ambush, the soldier, the amputation." Her eyes widened in surprise, something unreadable sparking in their clear depths. She released a heavy sigh, and he couldn't help but feel he had let her down somehow. "I'm sorry. I didn't realize they—"

She reached up and placed her fingers over his mouth, silencing him. Her gaze was steady as she watched him. Then she shook her head and gave him a ghost of a smile. "You didn't know, so it's not like it's your fault."

"You're not upset?"

"No, not really. I mean, a little, but not with you. I should have known better, especially with those two."

"I'm sorry. If I had known—" She cut him off again, this time with a kiss.

"We have four minutes left. Do you really want to waste them talking about this?"

No. God, no. He pulled her closer, his mouth hungry. Four minutes. Not nearly enough time. But he'd savor each one, even knowing how little sleep he'd get tonight, tossing and turning in frustration.

Thinking of everything he'd do to her when they got back home.

**

Dave came awake, instantly alert. He didn't move, barely breathed as he listened, seeking out whatever it was that had wakened him.

Shuffling steps out in the hallway. One person? No, two. Then another. Coming closer to his door. Hushed whispers, so quiet he couldn't make out the words. Then a knock at his door, sharp, determined.

Dave sat up in bed, reaching for his pants as CC opened the door and stepped into the room. Her parents were standing behind her, concern etched on their faces.

But it was CC he was focused on. CC, with her long hair mussed by sleep, her face pale, her eyes wide. Light from the hall reflected on her face, on the unnatural brightness shining in her eyes.

His gut clenched and his heart raced, heavy in his chest as a surge of adrenaline, of foreboding, flooded his veins. He looked down at the cordless phone in her shaking hand, looked back up at her. And he knew, even before she spoke the words.

"Dave, it's Jay. Angie's been an accident."

Chapter Twenty

Fear. Rage. Frustration. More fear.

The emotions tore through him, one after the other, nonstop. His stomach clenched, knotted, his mind spinning out of control, unable to focus.

Angie had been in an accident.

Dave kept repeating Jay's words to himself. She'll be okay. She'll be okay.

Bullshit. You didn't call someone at three in the morning for a fucking fender bender.

But Jay didn't go into much detail, Dave hadn't let him, just asked him which hospital as he threw his things into his bag and got dressed. Five minutes later, he was out the door, ready to tear off home, desperation filling him because it would take at least nine hours to get to the hospital if he broke every speed limit driving between here and home.

But he didn't drive.

Ed and Rob were waiting for them when they got outside, Ed's truck running, ready to go. CC had pushed him into the truck, not saying a word, and he hadn't been thinking clearly enough to argue. Thirty minutes later, they pulled into a small airport, Dave had no idea where and he didn't care, not when he saw the small jet waiting for them.

Less than two hours later, they landed at another small airport back home. They were now less than five minutes from the hospital, CC driving her car, lights and sirens splitting the pre-dawn darkness around them.

Dave didn't remember anything of the flight, nothing except CC's hand securely wrapped around his and her whispered words of reassurance. And Rob, seated across from them, looking nothing like the brother he had come to know.

He knew that his muddled mind would eventually put everything together and come up with questions, lots of questions. And he knew, without asking, without thinking, that they were breaking all kinds of rules.

And he didn't give a shit, not if it meant getting to Angie sooner.

CC tore into the parking lot of the ER, tires squealing. Dave had the door opened and was climbing out before she put the car in park. He knew they were right behind him, CC and Rob both, but he didn't stop, didn't wait as he pushed through the doors of the ER, cold desperation racing through him.

He went straight to the triage desk, barely acknowledging the nurse who greeted him with a small smile before telling him that Angie had been admitted and was already upstairs. Dave tore the paper with Angie's room number from the nurse's hand and kept going, cursing at the slowness of the elevator as it crawled to the fifth floor.

She'll be okay. She'll be okay.

He repeated the words to himself, then realized he was actually hearing them. CC was next to him, her hand resting on his arm, her face, drawn and pale, turned up to his. Dave clenched his jaw, swallowed, tried to nod.

Gave up and just pulled CC into his arms and held on, needing to feel her touch, to hear her reassuring words, to drink her willing strength.

The doors hissed open and he stepped out, kept going through the hallway, turning left then right, swearing at the absurdity of the maze that made it difficult to find the right wing, the right room. He pushed through another set of doors, to another hallway. And stopped.

A knot of people was gathered outside a room halfway down the hall, talking quietly or just standing around. His shift. Damn near his entire shift was here. His mind went blank, the scene completely throwing him as he tried to make sense of the familiar faces in such an unfamiliar place.

The mental vertigo lasted less than a second before things clicked and the world righted. His shift was here. Of course they'd be here. They were family. His. Jay's. Angie's.

He kept walking, his long legs tearing up the distance between them. He knew he talked to them, must have said something in response to whatever questions or comments were made. But his mind still wasn't completely registering things, not the way it should.

And then he was in Angie's room, his heart twisting, his gut knotting as he stopped at the foot of her bed. Her skin was pale, washed out against the stark white of the sheets and blanket covering her. Her left arm was wrapped in bandages, a sling holding it in place against her chest. A small trail of dried blood ran across the back of her hand, down to her fingers and nails.

Cuts and abrasions marred her face, a longer one on her left cheek stitched. Her lip was swollen and he could see that it had been split, that they had stitched it as well. Her eyes were closed, her head turned to the right. Dave watched as her chest rose and fell with each breath, short and slightly ragged instead of the deep breathing of healing sleep.

He swallowed and stepped closer to the bed, finally looking over at Jay. He was sitting to her right, bent over with his head resting against the bed, both hands clasped gently around Angie's.

Dave swallowed hard, anxiety still flowing through him. The fingers of icy dread that had squeezed his chest since getting the phone call eased, but just the slightest bit.

He must have made a noise, or maybe Jay could just sense him standing there, because the man lifted his head from the bed and turned toward him. His short blonde hair stood in disarray, the strands sticking up and out as if he had dragged his hands through them. Repeatedly. His gray eyes were bloodshot and lines of tension bracketed his mouth. His lips moved, as if he was trying to smile, but it turned into a grimace and he just shook his head, his worry and anxiety a reflection of Dave's own emotions.

"How is she?"

"They say she's going to be okay. Sprained wrist. Sprained knee. Concussion." Jay's voice was hoarse, ragged, as if he hadn't gotten much sleep. It finally registered in Dave's muddled mind that Jay was in uniform, his shirt wrinkled, unbuttoned and hanging open over his t-shirt. A set of turn-out pants sat in the corner, the suspenders tangled around the legs and boots, as if they had just been thrown there.

"What happened?"

"Hit and run. A truck nailed her broadside as she was heading home. They're still trying to figure out exactly what happened."

Dave nodded, swallowed again as he looked back at Angie, so still in the bed. So fragile. Fury tore through him at the thought of someone doing this to his sister. Doing it, then running away. But he clamped it down, pushed it away, knowing there was nothing he could do about it. For now.

"The son of a bitch hit her so hard, we had to cut her out." Jay's voice broke and he cleared his throat, looking away. Dave didn't miss his use of the word 'we', realized that Jay must have been on the call. But he didn't say anything, realized there was nothing he could say.

Angie shifted on the bed and moaned, a quiet, pitiful sound that tore through Dave. Her eyes fluttered open, blinking, then settled on Jay with a depth of feeling and emotion that even Dave could see from where he was standing. She blinked again then turned her head and looked at him, surprise in her eyes. She tried to smile, then winced as the movement pulled the stitches in her lip.

"What are you doing here?"

Dave stared at her, trying to comprehend the words, wondering if he had heard her correctly. "You really have to ask me that?"

She tried to smile again then turned to Jay. "You

look awful. Why don't you go get some coffee?"

Jay looked surprised at her words and looked like he was going to refuse. But she squeezed his hand, something unspoken passing between them, and he reluctantly stood up. He leaned over the bed and pressed a kiss to her forehead, something so tender in the action that Dave actually looked away.

Jay stopped next to him, his eyes so full of anxiety, concern, and love for his sister that Dave actually reached out and squeezed his shoulder.

Just one more apology he needed to make. But not now.

He stepped around the side of the bed and lowered himself into the chair Jay had just vacated then looked at his sister. Really looked. "How are you feeling?"

She shrugged, and Dave didn't miss the wince that accompanied it. "Like I've been hit by a truck."

"That's not even funny." He could see her trying to smile and felt the icy fingers loosen their grip from his heart a bit more.

"Stiff. Sore. My whole left side hurts."

"I bet it does." He hesitated, then reached out and closed his hand around hers, gently squeezing her fingers.

"Promise me you won't give Jay a hard time."

"Why would I do that?"

"Because I know you're still upset."

Dave tried to find something funny to say in response, something sarcastic that would alleviate her worry. But he couldn't. "I'm not upset. Not anymore. And you have more important things to worry about anyway."

She watched him, her dark eyes studying,

searching. He didn't know what she saw in his eyes, but it must have reassured her because she nodded then closed her eyes. She took a small breath then let it out, the sound tired, weary.

"He was pretty freaked out when he realized it was me."

"You remember what happened?"

She shook her head, frowning. "No. Not all of it. I remember headlights, but nothing after that. Not until I opened my eyes and saw Jay staring at me. I couldn't figure out why he was standing next to my car."

"Yeah, well." Dave cleared his throat and looked down at their joined hands, his sister's small and pale compared to his. He tried to imagine Jay's reaction at the wreck, how he must have felt when he saw it was Angie. The image was too clear, the emotion too real, because he knew what his own reaction would have been. "I'm glad he was there for you."

Angie didn't say anything, just squeezed his hand. Dave thought she must be drifting back off to sleep, knew that was the best thing for her, even though she'd be awakened by the nurses and checked on, repeatedly. But she stirred again and opened her eyes, a frown on her face.

"How did you get here so fast? I thought you were still in South Carolina."

"I was."

"Then how—"

"I'm still trying to figure that one out myself." Angie just watched him, her eyes boring into his long enough that he finally sighed and gave in. "Let's just say CC and her family must have some pretty nice connections."

"CC's here too?"

"And her brother. Out in the hall with everyone from work."

"Really? Why?"

"Why? Because everyone cares about you, kiddo. Don't be stupid."

"I'm not stupid. Just a little fuzzy." She took another breath, her eyes fluttering shut. "And stop calling me kiddo."

Dave smiled at the annoyance so clear in her tired voice, then cleared his throat against the thick emotion clogging it. "You're always going to be kiddo to me. You know that."

"Hm." Her chest rose and fell, the rhythm slow, steady, reassuring. Dave knew she was surrendering to sleep, surrendering to the slow healing process. He squeezed her hand once more, his voice barely above a whisper.

"Love you, kiddo."

A long minute went by, then Angie's fingers tightened around his, ever so slightly. "Love you back."

He smiled again at her slurred words, watched as she finally slipped into sleep. Her hand relaxed in his but he didn't let go, just sat by her side until Jay finally returned, looking only marginally better than he had when he left.

"How is she?"

"Sleeping. Which is what you need to do." Dave finally released Angie's hand and stood, offering the chair to Jay. But the man just stood there, his worried gaze fixed on the bed. Dave searched his mind, looking for something to say. Then a nurse entered the room, businesslike and efficient, and forced them out into the hallway, telling them Angie needed her rest. Her eyes finally softened, and then she reassured them they could come back in a few minutes—as long as they promised not to disturb her.

Dave glanced around the group of people in the hall, his eyes finally settling on CC standing off to the side, next to her brother. She came up to him, her arms sliding around his waist, holding him close. He closed his eyes and just held her, feeling her strength leach into him.

"How is she?"

"Okay. I think she's going to be okay."

She nodded against his chest, her arms tightening around him briefly before she stepped away. Worry creased her face, worry and something else he couldn't read as she glanced over her shoulder toward her brother.

"Dave, there's something you need to see."

The icy fear gripped him again, unexplained, unexpected. He looked down at CC then over to Rob. The man leaned against the wall, his face a blank mask, his eyes cold as he looked down at something in his hands.

A phone.

Dave's phone.

"No." Dave shook his head, denial and fear flooding him. CC bit her bottom lip, her wariness clear as she grabbed his hand. He shook his head again, pulling against CC, refusing to move. "No."

But CC gently tugged, forcing him to move, making him follow her until they stopped in front of Rob. The man held the phone out to him. Dave shook his head, willed his hand to stay at his side. But he had no control over it, watched in horror as he reached out to take the phone from Rob. Fear, dread, denial warred inside him. And fury, ice cold, blazing, almost debilitating.

"I don't think this was an accident." Rob's voice was low, the words clear, crisp, biting.

Dave kept shaking his head, not wanting to look, not able to stop himself from looking. He lowered his eyes and stared at the phone, his fingers cold and numb, his eyes seeing the text message on the screen even as his mind screamed in denial.

You shouldn't have left.

Chapter Twenty-One

CC leaned against the wall, her arms folded across her chest, a frown on her face. Tension, thick and heated, threatened to suffocate everyone in the small room.

The detective who had come to take the report. Bubby. Dave. Jay. Her.

The room was too damn small for all five of them. Throw in a table and some plastic chairs, and there was barely room for anyone to move.

Her eyes moved around the room, studying the other occupants, watching, assessing. The detective stood on one side of the table, looking frustrated, maybe just a little impatient. His questions had been asked and answered, his notes taken down. His last words rang hollow, empty, less than promising.

Yes, they'd put a trace on the call. No, he didn't expect them to find anything. Yes, there was a possibility the message and the accident were related. No, he didn't expect to be able to prove it, not with the information they had.

Which was damn little.

CC ground her teeth together, fighting the urge to go over and shove the detective in the chest, to push him against the wall, to make him do something. Anything. But she didn't, because she knew that was her own frustration speaking. She was a cop. Granted, a Flight Medic, but still a cop. And while detective work wasn't her specialty, she knew enough to realize that the guy was merely doing his job.

And that he was right. They had damn little to go on.

She looked over to Bubby, saw a similar frown on his own stark face. She had been surprised he had come with them, though she guessed it made sense, since he was the one who had pulled whatever strings he had to pull to get them here so quickly. The true extent of what he really did was still a mystery. After tonight, she didn't think she really wanted to know.

But she was counting on him now. Blind faith in her brother and his ability to find things that didn't exist reassured her. Maybe it wasn't logical. Maybe it wouldn't even help. But she was glad he was here.

He looked up from whatever he was reading on his phone and looked at her, his face now carefully blank, his gaze steady. She couldn't tell what he was thinking, saw no meaningful message in the look he was giving her. And she hoped that meant something.

She moved her gaze to Jay, surprised that the man had accompanied them. Then again, maybe not. His eyes were bloodshot, rimmed in red from worry and no doubt fatigue. His face was pale and drawn, a contrast to the rough stubble on his jaw, a darker blonde than his hair. Someone had told her that he had been on the engine that had responded to the accident, arriving before the medic unit. She could only imagine the emotion and thoughts that had run through his mind, because sometimes not even the best training in the world was enough to provide the emotional buffer you needed to distance yourself. And from the expression on his face, the weary set of his shoulders, it looked like whatever buffer he may have had was long gone.

Which left Dave.

She took a deep breath, readying herself before letting her gaze slide to him. He sat in one of the plastic chairs, his elbows propped on the table, his head hanging in his hands. Regret and guilt poured from him in waves, his dejection a living thing for everyone in the room to see and feel. Her heart squeezed and her throat tightened as she watched him, and she wished there was something she could do, something she could say, to make his pain go away. Wished there was some way she could convince him that this wasn't his fault.

He wasn't ready to hear that, though. She didn't know if he'd ever be ready to hear it.

Dave had said very little after seeing the text message, his last denial ripped from his throat in a voice that still chilled her. Bubby had found this room, she didn't know how, and had led them in here to wait for the detective. Dave had answered the questions, his voice devoid of all emotion, his answers mostly monosyllables. CC had jumped in, adding details when needed, then had to snap her own mouth shut when the detective coolly reminded her that she wasn't the one being questioned. Without saying a word, she reached into her back pocket and pulled out her wallet, flipping it open to show her badge.

The detective hadn't said anything else to her since then.

He pushed off the wall he had been leaning against and closed his notepad. "I'll pull the other reports, get everything together and look them over. But I'll be honest, I don't think there's much we'll be able to find out."

"So that's it? You just walk away and pretend you'll get back to us?" Anger dripped from Jay's voice and CC knew that the tension, the worry, the fear from the last few hours were taking their toll, that the powder keg of emotion filling the room was dangerously close to exploding.

The detective didn't bother to answer Jay as he walked toward the door. He stopped, turned around, his eyes finally settling on Bubby. "I'll be in touch."

"What fucking bullshit. Seriously, that's it?" Jay paced to the far end of the room, his steps short, angry. He stopped, looked down at Dave then over at CC. "They're really not going to do anything, are they?"

"There's nothing they can do." Dave's voice was hollow, lifeless. Like he had fallen into some forsaken pit of despair and lost the will to find his way out. CC's heart clenched again. She wanted to say something, do something. But she couldn't, because what he said was true.

"Don't say that! There has to be something. Some sick bastard damn near killed your sister and that's all you can say? Bullshit! Somebody needs to do something!" Jay's angry voice bounced off the walls, as if sheer volume could make something happen. Dave flew out of the chair, throwing it behind him with such force that it dented the drywall. His face was red, his fists clenched as he stepped closer to Jay. CC moved forward, afraid of what was to come, but Bubby stopped her with one hand.

"Don't you think I know that? Don't you think I'd fucking do something if I could? I want to kill the fucking bastard with my bare hands but I can't because I. Don't. Know. Who. He. Is."

The two men stared off against each other, both of them looking as if they were ready to come to blows. Then just as quickly as his outburst struck, all the fight seemed to drain from Dave. His shoulders slumped in defeat and he turned away from all of them. He ran his hands through his hair then locked his hands behind his neck, staring up at the ceiling. CC couldn't see his face but knew his expression was one of despair, of desperation, because she could feel those emotions flowing from him, as clear and biting as if they were her own.

"I don't know what to do. I don't know who this guy is or what he wants. It feels like I've been facing off against a ghost for almost nine months now, and I don't know what to do."

"Why didn't you say something? Why didn't you tell us?" Jay stepped closer to Dave, leaned up against the wall so he could see him. "Everybody figured something was up. You should have let us know, maybe we could have helped."

"What was I supposed to say? 'Hey guys, I've been getting these really weird texts that have been vaguely threatening from someone somewhere but I don't know who because whenever I send a text back, it never goes through.' What the hell good would that have done?"

"I don't know. Nothing. Everything."

CC glanced over at Jay and heard his unfinished

thought: that if he had known, maybe Angie wouldn't be in the hospital right now. She wasn't sure why he didn't say it, but was thankful he didn't—even though she was pretty sure Dave had already thought the same thing himself.

"So keep replying to him." Rob finally spoke, his voice calm, reasoning. Dave turned around and faced her brother, his dark eyes nothing but hollows in his face, his shoulders slumped in resignation.

"Why? They bounce back. Every time."

"He's escalating. Maybe he wants a reply now, an acknowledgement."

"What good would that do? Will it help find him?"

"Maybe. Maybe not. Maybe it'll push him into doing something else, maybe you can convince him to meet you."

"Bubby, is that even a good idea?"

He looked over at her and shrugged. "It's the only one I have for now." But there was something in his eyes, something lurking in their depths that said he wasn't telling her everything. And she had never placed so much faith in her brother as she did at that moment.

She walked over to Dave and held out her hand. "Let me see your phone."

He pulled it from his pocket and gave it to her without saying a word. She took it and tapped the text message icon, bringing up the single line from the unknown sender.

You shouldn't have left.

She stared at it a few seconds, trying to put herself in Dave's mind, trying to phrase a response that would come from him. Her thumb tapped against the screen but she paused before hitting send, looked back at Bubby. He nodded, and she pressed the button.

I'm here now. Come get me.

Silence filled the room as they waited and CC wondered what would happen if they actually received a message back. Would it be that easy? Was Bubby right, thinking this guy would want some acknowledgement of what he'd done?

If he had done it. They still had to accept the possibility that it was just coincidence. But CC shook her head. No, maybe the police had to accept that, but there was no doubt in her mind that everything was connected. No doubt in any of their minds.

The phone beeped, startling her enough that she almost dropped it. Dave's face paled and he leaned against the wall, as if he no longer had the strength to stand. Bubby moved closer, looking over her shoulder as she tapped the screen.

Message Failed.

"Fuck." Her fingers tightened around the phone when all she wanted to do was throw it against the wall.

"Now what?" The question came from Jay, who looked nearly as desperate as Dave. CC didn't have an answer and turned to her brother once more.

He reached around her and took the phone, dropping it into his own pocket. The move surprised her and she was ready to ask him what he was doing, but he shook his head. "We wait."

"What about Angie?" Dave looked up, his gaze moving between Bubby and her. "I don't want anything happening to her, she can't be left alone."

"She's not going to be alone. I'll be with her." Jay's voice was hard, his expression carved from stone.

"And what about when we're working? Who's going to be with her then?"

"I've got vacation built up. I'll use it all if I have

to."

"Jay, that's not good enough! He knows where I live, he knows where Angie works. And we don't even know how long this could go on for. It's already been going on for almost nine months!"

"Two weeks." Bubby looked between the two men, his face calm, thoughtful. "Give it two weeks, and I'll find a place for Angie and Jay to stay."

"A safe place?" CC tried to keep the skepticism from her voice, wondering how even her brother could guarantee that.

"Yeah, I'm thinking they'll be pretty safe at Mom and Dad's. Especially if Tim's there."

"Rob, no. That's—"

"Actually a pretty good idea." CC cut Dave's complaint short.

"It's too much. I can't ask you to do that."

"You're not asking, are you? So unless you have a better idea, it's set. I'll make the arrangements." Rob watched Dave, waiting for an objection that wouldn't come, then turned to Jay. "You'll both be fine there. And it'll give Angie time to rest, recuperate."

Bubby was worse than a steamroller in action, making decisions and issuing orders, completely in charge. CC reached out and closed her hand around his wrist, stopping him when he would have walked past her. Yes, she had complete faith in her brother, but he wasn't infallible.

"And what if nothing happens in two weeks? What then?"

He looked down at her, his eyes briefly warming before changing back to their cool, professional detachment. "Then we figure it out then. CC, I'm working on the fly here. You have to give me some time, okay? I'll make sure things work out." He leaned down and brushed a kiss against the top of her head, like he used to do when they were kids. "I need to go do a few things. I'll meet you back at your place."

"Wait. You don't have a car, remember?"

"It's already taken care of." He stepped past her, closing the door with a soft click behind him. She blew out a breath and tucked the hair behind her ears, wondering—not for the first time—the true extent of what Bubby did for a living.

"I'm going back to Angie's room, see how she's doing." Jay started past Dave then stopped and placed a hand on his shoulder. "We'll get this figured out, okay?"

Dave didn't respond, did nothing more than briefly nod his head. CC figured it was nothing more than an empty gesture, that he wasn't really agreeing, wasn't believing. Jay walked past, giving her a nod of acknowledgement as he left.

And then it was just the two of them. Alone.

Dave leaned his head against the wall and closed his eyes, tension echoing in every tight line of his body. And CC knew that, for the moment at least, Dave felt as if he was the only person in the room. His loneliness, his guilt and desperation, surrounded her, filling her with sadness, filling her with her own desperation.

She closed the few feet separating them and wrapped her arms around his waist, stepping close, holding him tightly as if she could take his pain and turmoil away by simply touching him, simply by sheer force of her will. She rested her head against his chest, the sound of his heart solid and steady beneath her ear. She didn't speak, because there was nothing she could say. No words she could utter that would make any of this better.

Long minutes went by before his arms closed around her, tight, as if she was a lifeline he couldn't let go. His chest heaved under the force of his ragged breathing, his heart skipping a few beats then pounding under her ear.

"Oh God, CC, what am I going to do? What did I do to make this bastard hate me so much that he'd go after my sister?" Emotion clogged his throat, his words thick, choked. And still she said nothing, just held him, knowing that he wasn't expecting a response. "I don't know how to fight him. I don't know what to do."

Time stilled. Or maybe it sped up, CC wasn't sure. They just stood there, holding onto each other, CC praying that she could offer Dave strength, if nothing else. She wished she had words she could offer him, guarantees she could make that would make things better. But she didn't. All she could do was hold him as his breathing grew harsher under her ear, as emotion shook him as the reality of what was going on sunk in.

All she could do was hold him tight, and hope that he knew she was there for him.

Chapter Twenty-Two

The sun was high, nearly straight above them in the cool October air. The parking lot was busy, cars vying for spots, people milling around. Dave looked around, confused, trying to remember why they were in this particular lot. This wasn't where they had parked.

CC walked ahead of him, glancing back over her shoulder once to smile. He tried to smile back but his lips wouldn't cooperate. Something felt wrong. A man brushed by him, hurrying past. Then he stopped, turned back to Dave.

You shouldn't have left.

The man grinned, his face featureless except for that grin. Something was wrong. The grin was wrong. Cold, twisted, not really a grin at all. But the man had already turned back around, his steps hurried as he approached CC.

Something was wrong.

Dave opened his mouth, tried to call out a warning, but CC didn't hear him. The man was behind her now, his arm raised, like he was waving to someone. Sunlight flashed off metal as he brought his arm down in a wide arc—

Dave bolted upright, his heart pounding in his chest as he sucked in huge gulps of air. He looked around, his eyes squinting against the light spilling through the window.

"Fuck."

He swung his legs to the side of the bed then rested his head in his hands. Tremors ran through his body and he closed his eyes, trying to calm his breathing. Trying to calm his soaring pulse.

"Fuck."

He was at CC's house, in her bed, because she had insisted he try to get some rest. He had no idea what time it was, no idea how long he had slept, only knew that he felt battered, worn out, exhausted.

But not exhausted enough to prevent dreaming. And he didn't need a shrink to explain that little nightmare. No, he was quite capable of figuring that one out all on his own.

Footsteps padded lightly across the hardwood floors of the hallway, stopping at the door of the room. Dave looked up as CC leaned against the doorframe, her long hair loose around her shoulders, her delicate brows lowered above clear hazel eyes. Her lips were slightly pursed, concern and worry clear on her face.

"How are you feeling?" Her voice was low, a little rusty, as if she hadn't spoken in a while.

He nodded, shook his head, finally shrugged then swallowed, his throat dry and scratchy. Not from getting sick, not from lack of use, but from too much emotion. He was almost afraid to speak, afraid of what his voice would sound like.

Afraid of embarrassing himself again. One emotional breakdown a year was more than enough, and he had already had that in the hospital earlier this morning.

"Hungover. Beat-up."

One corner of her mouth turned up, not quite a smile. She stayed where she was, though, just leaning against the doorframe, a picture of forced casualness in her sweatpants and baggy t-shirt. Part of him was glad she stayed where she was, giving him enough space to collect himself. Another part wanted nothing more than to pull her into his arms, to feel the comfort and reassurance of her touch.

But he didn't say anything, just ran his hands over his face, as if he could brush away the nightmare of the last twenty-four hours.

The nightmare that had sent him bolting upright from restless sleep.

"You feel up to eating something? Bubby stopped by the store, picked up some cheese and crackers and stuff."

Dave shook his head again. "Not just yet, no. Is he out there?"

"No, he left again. Don't ask where, he didn't say, just said he'd be back tonight." She tried smiling again, with the same success as before. "And to lock the doors, and to have my gun within reach."

She may have meant it as a joke, as a dig against over-protective big brothers, but her words sent a chill through Dave. It was a stark reminder of the seriousness of the situation, of the potential danger facing him from some unknown threat.

A reminder of the brief nightmare.

Dave pushed himself off the bed, looking around

for his t-shirt. "CC, I need to leave, I can't stay here."

"What are you talking about?"

There, over on the chair. Neatly folded on top of his jeans. He walked over and grabbed his clothes with still-shaking hands. Dropped them on the floor then bent down to pick them up. "I can't stay here. I should have never dragged you into this, should have never let you talk me into staying here. You've already done enough. I'm not going to be responsible for anything happening to you."

He fumbled with the shirt, trying to get his hands to work, to cooperate. But they wouldn't, they were still shaking as images of CC being attacked played in his mind.

"Must have been some nightmare."

Her softly-spoken words froze him in place, the shirt falling to the floor once more. He swallowed then turned to look at her, wondering what she was talking about, afraid of what he may have said in his sleep. She watched him for a few seconds then shrugged.

"I heard you yell my name, figured you must have been dreaming."

"Yeah. Yeah, dreaming. Sure." And wasn't that just what he needed, on top of everything else? It was bad enough he was beginning to fall apart, he didn't need anyone actually witnessing it. CC had already witnessed enough this morning.

She watched him for another long second then let out a heavy sigh and pushed away from the doorframe. She leaned down and picked his shirt up from the floor, but instead of handing it to him, she tossed it back on the chair.

"If you're going to start worrying about the fact that I know you had a nightmare, don't. If it really bothers you, I'll tell you some of mine and we'll be even."

"CC—"

"And as for everything else, I call bullshit. You didn't drag me into this. In fact, if I recall, I'm the one who dragged you." She stepped closer, pointing her index finger in the direction of his chest, like she was ready to jab him.

"CC—"

This time her finger did jab him, effectively silencing him. "You're not putting me in danger, and you're not responsible if anything happens to me. I can take care of myself, remember?"

"But I am—"

Her finger jabbed him again, twice, right in the middle of his chest. "And if you want to be hard-headed about it, you might want to remember that your truck is still in South Carolina. Are you planning to walk home, Big Guy?"

"Fuck." She was right, he was at her mercy. For now. But that didn't change things, didn't alleviate the sickening knowledge that if anything happened to her, he would be responsible.

He looked down at her upturned face, at the stubbornness and determination lighting her eyes. He brushed her hand away from his chest and cupped her face between his hands. "CC, I don't want anything to happen to you, I can't be responsible for that."

"Nothing is going to happen."

"Like nothing was going to happen to Angie?" Damn his voice for breaking, damn the emotion that clogged his throat.

CC's eyes softened as she stared up at him, warm and understanding. And still stubborn. She placed the palm of her hand over his heart, tried to smile. "Dave, you can't wrap everyone around you in bubble wrap and lock them up, trying to keep them safe. It doesn't work that way. You know that."

"Not everyone. Just the people I care about."

Something flashed in her eyes, something warm and intoxicating, but only briefly. Just long enough for the worry inside him to subside, if only for a minute. She wrapped her hands around his wrists, slowly pushing them away from her face.

"Thank you. I care about you, too. But you have to stop worrying, Dave. We'll get this figured out." She slid her arms around his waist and held him, her head against his chest, her body pressed tightly, trustingly, against him.

He took a deep breath, swallowed again, surprised that his throat no longer felt quite as tight, quite as scratchy. Then he wrapped his arms around her and held her. Just held her.

"We'll figure this out together, okay?" Her words were softly spoken, her breath warm against his chest as she placed a kiss over his heart. He looked down at her, saw reassurance and trust in her eyes.

And he suddenly needed more. Needed to feel the reassurance in a more basic way. He lowered his head, his mouth closing over hers, gently at first, hesitant and unsure. But her response was immediate, eager, unleashing something primal within him.

He delved his tongue into her mouth, tasting fiery sweetness. And he needed more. Now.

He grabbed the hem of her shirt and tore it over her head, tossing it somewhere behind her before pushing the sweatpants down her legs, past her hips and thighs. His hand drifted back up her leg, slid between her thighs, his finger stroking her clit. She moaned, thrusting her hips toward him, her hand closing around his wrist, guiding him, showing him where to touch.

She moaned again then reached for the waistband of his briefs, snagging the elastic with her fingers as she pulled them down. Her hand closed over him, squeezing, stroking his hard length from base to tip.

"CC." Her name was nothing more than a growl ripped from his throat. He wanted—needed—now. He walked her toward the bed, not stopping until the backs of her legs hit the mattress and she fell backwards.

Her hair tumbled around her shoulders, her full breasts thrust forward, rising up and down with each harsh breath. Dave grabbed her sweatpants, yanking them off and tossing them to the floor as he stepped out of his briefs. He kicked them away then fell on top of CC, bracing his weight on his hands as his mouth closed over hers once more. Hot, greedy, desperate.

She shifted under him, placing her heels on the mattress, opening her legs for him.

"CC..."

Her hands gripped his ass, the nails biting into his flesh as her teeth nipped at his lip. "Now."

Dave plunged into her, hard, deep, burying himself in her wet heat. He wanted, needed.

Out. In, hard, fast. Thrusting into her, needing to lose himself.

Needing to find himself.

Again, harder, faster.

Her nails raked his skin, her hips thrusting against him, meeting him, matching his rhythm. He clung to her, his mouth hard and demanding, relentless.

His hips thrust against her, plunging into her, over and over. Desperate, seeking. She tightened around him, hot, wet. Her teeth nipped at his lip then she threw her head back, her mouth parted, her eyes closed as her orgasm ripped through her, his name a low moan, called over and over.

And it wasn't enough, would never be enough. He pounded into her, harder, faster, deeper. Desperate still. His balls tightened, almost painfully. Then his own climax tore through him, sharp, primal, filling her.

Losing himself. Finding himself.

His chest constricted, each breath harsh, ragged, as he sank onto her. Her hands roamed the flesh of his back, his ass, her touch softer now. Comforting and reassuring.

Time slowed, the only sounds their mingled breathing, the pounding of their hearts, each echoing the other. Seconds ticked by, marked by each beat, faster, fast, finally slowing.

Dave fought to catch his breath as realization slammed into him.

The realization of how he felt.

The realization of what he wanted.

The realization of how hard he had used her. He pushed up on his hands, his eyes closed, afraid to look at her. "Christ. CC, I'm sorry, I didn't mean—"

He felt her mouth on his, silencing him, reassuring him. Soft, tender.

"Don't. There's nothing to apologize for." She traced his lips with her fingers and he opened his eyes, looking down at her. Tenderness and understanding filled her eyes. And emotion, deep and undefined, but still filling him with warmth. He lowered his mouth to hers, sweet, gentle. Then he pulled away and shifted, heard her moan as he rolled off of her.

He slid further up the bed, pulling her with him so their legs weren't hanging off the edge. He wrapped his arm around her, tucking her against his side, and just held her.

He closed his eyes and drifted off, knowing that a lifetime with the woman in his arms would never be enough.

Chapter Twenty-Three

Orange streaks spread across the horizon, mixing with the deep purple of twilight as the minutes crept forward. CC shifted on the wicker loveseat, curling her legs underneath her, and stared out at the reflection of colors on the water.

But she wasn't really seeing them, wasn't really aware of anything around her, not consciously. Her mind was on the man in her room, his body relaxed in slumber, seeking the peace he couldn't find while wake.

She took a deep breath then looked down at her hands, folded in her lap, her knuckles white from being clenched so hard. Clenched because even now, hours later, her hands were still shaking.

And she hated herself for it.

Hated herself because they shouldn't be shaking. She shouldn't be worried, shouldn't be mentally berating herself. No, she should be happy, should be smiling, despite everything else that was going on.

Something had happened, something profound and earth-shattering, when Dave had made love to her a few hours ago. Maybe 'made love' was too gentle a term. It was a coupling. A primal, basic coming-together, born of need and desperation, need for reassurance on his part.

A need to comfort, to give that reassurance on her part.

But it had become so much more and she was still trying to deal with the earth-shattering effects. Because she had realized, with horrifying clarity, that she had fallen in love with him.

Not just cared deeply. No, she had already realized that, had no problem with that at all. She liked the Big Guy, really liked him. Liked teasing him, liked drawing out his rare smiles and rare laughter. She had fun with him, enjoyed spending time with him. So yeah, she had no problem with admitting she cared about him.

But falling in love with him? That hadn't been in her plans—not that she really had any plans. And now she had no idea what to do, no idea what she wanted to do.

What the hell did she know about falling in love? Nothing, absolutely nothing. And it terrified her.

"Want some company?"

She looked over to see Bubby step out onto the porch, a bottle of beer in one hand and a glass of white wine in the other. He held the glass out to her then took a seat in the overstuffed wicker chair to her left, not bothering to wait for her invitation.

Probably because he knew she'd say no.

She gave him a pointed look then sipped the wine, her gaze drifting back out to the water. Bubby watched her. She could feel his penetrating eyes boring a hole into her but she didn't turn back to look at him. Maybe he'd get the point and realize she wanted to be left alone, that she had too much on her mind right now and wasn't in the mood for company.

"I know that deep, serious look. You're heavy in thought about something, and I don't think it has anything to do with threatening text messages. Want to talk about it?"

"Not really, no."

Bubby actually chuckled, damn him. She gave him a look that let him know, loud and clear, that she wasn't amused. She took another sip of wine then changed the subject.

"What'd you do with Dave's phone?"

"I put it on the kitchen counter."

"That's not what I meant and you know it. What'd you do with it when you took it at the hospital?"

Bubby didn't answer, just looked at her, his face a blank mask. She sighed and looked away, knowing she wouldn't get an answer. Not now, probably not ever.

"He's a nice guy. I like him, despite what's going on right now."

"Hm."

"Hm? That's all you can say?"

"Okay. Hm. I like him, too. Is that better?"

Bubby laughed again. "Tim and I were teasing him last night, telling him we thought it was funny that you had him all tied up in knots. Looks like he's not the only one tied up."

"Last night?" CC frowned, then shook her head in surprise when she realized Bubby must be talking about when the three of them had been hanging out by the fire. Last night, back home. In South Carolina. God, had it really just been last night? So much had happened since then.

And then the rest of his words sunk in and she

whirled around to face him, frowning. "What's that supposed to mean?"

"It means just what you think it means. He's not the only one tied up in knots."

"I have no idea what you're talking about."

"Don't you?" He watched her, his eyes quiet and intense. She turned away before he could see too much. "Mom and Dad like him, too. You guys make a good couple."

"Hm." And she so didn't want to talk about this. Not now, and certainly not with her older brother. In fact, she didn't want to talk about it at all. With anyone. Not even herself.

"What's the matter, CC? Thought you were immune?"

"And again, I have no idea what you're talking about."

"There's nothing wrong with falling in love, especially not with someone who feels the same way."

"Bubby, you have no idea what you're talking about. And you're seeing things that aren't there."

"Really?" Impatience edged his voice but she refused to look at him. "What I'm seeing is a girl who's so bent on proving herself to the world, who's convinced herself that she doesn't need anyone. A girl who thinks that admitting she wants someone in her life is a weakness. It doesn't work that way, CC."

She whipped her head around and fixed him with an angry glare, afraid to admit his words were too close to the truth. "What the hell do you know about it?"

A shadow passed through his eyes, dark, dangerous. Haunted. He blinked and the shadow was gone, replaced by a calculated coolness that sent a chill through her.

"Enough, CC. I know enough. Be smart for once and listen to me. Don't throw away a chance at being happy by confusing need with weakness, or you'll regret it." Anger flared in his eyes, followed by another haunted shadow that he quickly blinked away. The muscle in his jaw twitched and he finally looked away.

CC said nothing, her mind too tangled to form a coherent sentence. Was her brother talking from experience? She thought so, but she had no idea who he might be talking about. And it didn't matter, because whatever he was talking about didn't concern her. She wasn't trying to prove anything to anybody. And she wasn't confusing need with weakness.

She didn't *need*, period.

She turned away from her brother and looked back out over the water, the sky no longer filled with blazing color. Twilight had settled in and was already giving way to night as the air turned just a little cooler.

CC told herself it had everything to do with the sun going down and nothing to do with Bubby's certain words. No, not his words. His warning.

"I'm going to throw the pizza in the oven. Why don't you go wake sleeping beauty? Then we can talk some more, come up with a plan."

"Sleeping beauty's awake." Dave's quiet voice came from behind her and she jumped, startled, then turned to face him. Had he heard what they were talking about? And even if he did, would he understand?

The lines around his eyes were soft, his face relaxed, as if the sleep had allowed him to release some of his tension and worry. No, he hadn't heard them, of that she was sure.

Bubby stood up, smiling as he looked Dave over.

"Well, at least you look a little more human now. Want a beer?"

"Yeah, thanks."

Bubby walked by him, disappearing into the house. Dave glanced over at her for a second then sat in the chair her brother had just left. She watched him, surprised. Told herself she wasn't disappointed that he hadn't sat next to her.

He stretched his legs out then ran his hands through his hair, like he was still trying to wake up. His hair was damp around the edges, his face freshly scrubbed. CC realized he must have washed up, or at least rinsed his face with water.

She let her eyes wander over him, forcing herself to remain detached, to just observe. He was wearing an old gray t-shirt, the material thin from wear, the sleeves tight around his well-defined arms. The black sweatpants were worn as well, slightly faded and loose on him. Her gaze drifted lower, finally resting on his strong bare feet, and she surprised herself by actually grinning. Not because of his feet, but because his outfit matched hers, exactly. Bare feet and all.

She hid her smile behind the wine glass and looked away before he caught her staring. Then she realized what was happening and her smile died. Her heart pounded in her chest, warmth filling her just from watching him. And she thought she could be detached?

Then she realized she had been lying. She could tell herself she didn't need, period, but it was nothing more than a lie. She may not want to need, but she did. And she had no idea what to do about it. No idea what she wanted to do about it.

And she'd take the complications of Dave's anonymous threats a hundred times over the complications of what her heart was telling her.

"You shouldn't have let me sleep so late."

She turned at the sound of Dave's voice, felt the warmth build in her chest again and tried to push it away. "You needed your rest. Sometimes it's best just to listen to your body."

"Maybe. Except now I'll probably be up all night."

"You might surprise yourself." Bubby came back in, two bottles in his hand. He handed one to Dave, then sat in the chair opposite him. "They tried running a trace on the message but no luck. Not that we expected any differently."

"Of course not, that would be too easy. What the hell does this guy do, buy throwaway phones in bulk?" CC had meant the comment sarcastically and was surprised at the look Bubby gave her.

"We're actually looking into that. Do I think we'll find anything? No. But it can't hurt."

"'We'? What do you mean, 'we'?"

"Not 'we' like you're thinking. I'm not involved in any of this, remember? Doesn't mean I can't make a few calls, drop a few suggestions. So yeah, they're looking into that, but I don't expect anything to come of it."

"Then I'm back to just waiting, and hoping one day whoever is doing this responds back." Dave looked down at the bottle in his hand, frowning. "Which means this could go on forever. There hasn't been any rhyme or reason to the texts. No special days, no special times. I've gotten two in one week, then nothing for more than a month. What the hell am I supposed to do?"

"Wait. For now. I still say he's escalating, and that something is going to happen soon."

"So I'm just supposed to stop everything, keep looking over my shoulder?"

"For now. I know it's not what you want to hear, but I think that's your best option. You can stay here, I know CC won't mind."

Dave glanced over at her then looked back at her brother, shaking her head. "No, I can't stay here. That puts CC at risk. Not to mention that I do have a job. I'm not taking off work, not letting this guy force me into hiding."

CC ignored the stab of disappointment that flashed through her, even though what he said made sense. Even though he had already said he was afraid of putting her in danger. She looked at Dave, then at Bubby.

"He's right, you know. Not about staying here, we can talk about that later. But he can't just shut himself in. He has to go back to work. So do I. You, too, Bubby. There's got to be something better."

Frustration was clear on his face and she knew he didn't like it any better than she did. Any better than Dave did, for that matter. "Well right now, I don't have anything better. Nothing, that is, except a warning to just make damn sure you're aware of what's going on around you."

As far as reassurances went, it sucked. But she couldn't say anything, because he was right. There was nothing else to do, not with what they had so far.

The tinny sound of a timer dinging broke the silence around them. Bubby placed his bottle on the table, banging it just a little too hard, then pushed himself out of the chair. "I'll go get the pizza."

CC watched him leave, torn between offering to help, or leaving him alone. Considering how hard he slammed the bottle against the table, she figured he wanted to be left alone. She raised the wine glass to her mouth and sipped, her eyes resting on Dave. He looked up and their gazes met, heat and awareness flashing between them.

"You can stay here, you know."

"Yeah, I know."

"I think you should."

"Do you?" His gaze pierced hers, searching, serious, quiet. She forced herself not to squirm under the scrutiny and wondered again if he had heard them talking earlier, wondered if she had been wrong in thinking he hadn't.

She looked away and licked her lips, her mouth suddenly dry. She swallowed, then looked back at him. "Yeah, I do."

And God help her, it was the truth. She did want him to stay. Wanted to sleep in his arms each night, wake in his arms each morning, laugh and talk with him each day. Yes, she wanted all of those things. She wanted him.

She just didn't want to *need* him.

Dave took a swallow of beer, watching her over the bottle, his eyes never leaving hers. "Since I have no way of getting home right now, I guess I'm at your mercy. At least until I get some other transportation so I can work on Sunday. Until then, I guess I'm staying."

CC ignored the little jump of excitement and anticipation in her chest and just nodded. Nodded, and tried not to smile.

She was a hypocrite, a liar.

And she wondered exactly who she was lying to when she told herself she didn't need him.

Chapter Twenty-Four

"You okay?"

"Yeah. Fine." Dave slammed the back door of the medic then walked around the front, slamming the passenger door after he climbed in. Jimmy got into the driver's seat and closed his own door then started the engine, shooting Dave a cautious look before he pulled away from the ER.

And wisely said nothing.

Dave was not fine. In fact, he was anything but. He was tired, pissed, frustrated. And impatient as hell.

Might as well throw in confused and irritated.

He hadn't been sleeping well the last week, not since getting back from South Carolina. He kept checking his phone, looking for text messages, afraid he'd miss something.

Kept wondering when the bastard was going to send him another message, kept waiting for it.

And nothing. Not since that message the night at the hospital. Dave had even sent replies, over and over.

I'm here now. Come get me.

Every single one had failed to send.

His patience was shot. His nerves were shot. At least he had something to keep his mind off things when he was working. Except when he had time to think, which was between every call. Hell, even sometimes on the call. Like now, when he snapped at Jimmy.

He just wanted it to end, didn't know how much longer he could go without snapping for real. Today was Tuesday, their first night in. What the hell was he going to do Thursday morning, when he had off for four days? Sit around and wait?

Not like he had much choice.

At least Angie was safe. She and Jay were staying at the Covey's house and from what he had been told, she was recovering well. Joyce and Ed were both spoiling her, and Jay never left her side.

Dave had to take Rob's word for it, because he was told not to call her.

Just in case.

So he didn't. Just in case.

And for as bad as all that was, he had convinced himself that he could handle it, because he knew CC would be right there with him. That had been Thursday afternoon, before everything started falling apart.

And he still had no idea what the hell was going on. Something had changed. He didn't know what. He didn't know why. He didn't know how. But he had a pretty good idea of when.

Right after he pinned CC to the bed and used her to forget, to comfort himself, to find comfort in her. After he tried losing himself in her.

No, he *had* lost himself in her. In more ways than one. He realized what he was feeling went beyond casual interest, beyond whatever informal relationship he had thought they had. Yeah, way beyond. And he had thought, would have sworn, that he had seen something similar in CC's eyes that afternoon.

Until he woke up that evening, and realized something had changed.

They talked, they hung out, she did her best to make him smile or even laugh, to keep his mind off things. And he lost himself in her each night, fell asleep with her body curled next to his.

But something had changed. She was there, but she wasn't, not like she had been. And every time he gazed at her, whenever he thought he saw emotion in her eyes, she'd blink or look away then smile and make some joke, deflecting whatever he had been about to say.

At least he could be grateful for the fact that he hadn't been a complete moron and told her he loved her, because wouldn't that have been perfect? He wasn't stupid, he knew what she was doing. Pulling away, at least emotionally.

Which meant she didn't feel the same way. Or she didn't want to feel the same way. At this point, he didn't know which was worse. And on top of everything else, he didn't think he could play emotional tag.

He didn't want to play emotional tag. He couldn't, not with everything else going on.

Which left him absolutely nowhere, with no idea what to do next.

And he wasn't sure how much longer he could deal with it. All of it.

The radio came to life, jarring him back to reality. "Dispatch to Medic 14."

Dave reached for the mike, brought it to his

mouth. "Medic 14. Go."

"Medic 14. Respond 10-50 PI, possible rescue. 83 Northbound between Exits 20 and 21. Rescue assignment being dispatched. Reports of a car overturned. Do you copy, Medic 14?"

"Medic 14 copy. Responding." Dave tossed the mike back onto the console then reached above him and palmed the light switches. Jimmy hit the siren and did a sharp turn to change directions. His partner looked over at him, his gaze speculative, a grin on his face showing that damn dimple.

"What is it Jimmy?"

"Nothing. Just hoping that if it is a rescue, they let you at the car. Maybe you can take out whatever's up your ass on the car and be done with it."

"Bite me, Jimmy."

As it turned it, it was nothing more than a door pop with the patient complaining of neck and back pain. Followed by a call for chest pains, then another for a nose bleed. One call after another, so that by the time he pulled into his driveway the next morning, he was tired. Bone-weary tired.

Which hopefully meant he'd actually sleep.

He climbed out of the rental car with a groan then slammed the door shut. Dave had no idea where the car came from and didn't care. He only knew the damn thing was too small for his large frame and that he wanted his truck back.

Hell, he wanted his life back.

He let himself in the front door then frowned as stale air and silence greeted him. He dropped his bag in the living room then walked through to the kitchen, pausing only long enough to open windows as he went by them.

He opened the refrigerator, looking for something to drink, and frowned when he pulled out the milk. Six days past its expiration date, the gallon jug already had clumps floating in it. He made a face and put it back then scowled at the nearly empty shelves.

The refrigerator fairy had obviously failed to show since he had left last Monday. He shook his head and grabbed a beer from the bottom shelf, then twisted off the cap and walked over to the sliding doors leading out back. He tilted his head and took a long swallow, figuring what the hell. It wasn't like he was going anywhere except straight to sleep until it was time for his shift anyway.

The phone vibrated against his side and his heart kicked in the middle of his chest. He reached down, wondering if this was it, then released the breath he'd been holding when he saw CC's name on the screen.

"Hey."

"Hey Big Guy. Were you in the mood for breakfast? I can have it waiting for you when you get here."

He cringed at her bright voice, thinking it was too bright. Too forced. "Um, no, sorry. I'm already home."

There was a pause, followed by "Oh." Was it his imagination, or did she sound disappointed?

"We ran our asses off last night. I was just going to crash until it was time to go back in."

"Aww. Poor Big Guy. Guess you had to actually work, huh?" Her clear laugh came through the phone and he pictured her standing in her small kitchen, wearing baggy sweatpants and a t-shirt, leaning against the door as she looked out over the water. He wondered why he had even remotely thought she sounded disappointed.

"Yeah, guess so." He took a swallow of beer, his taste buds grimacing at the bitterness so early in the morning. "Maybe tomorrow?"

There was a slight pause before she laughed again, a little softer, a little shorter this time. "No can do, Big Guy. It's my turn to save lives tomorrow."

"Oh."

Silence stretched between them, moving to the awkward zone. Dave cleared his throat, searching for something to say. But then he heard CC's laughter again, maybe just a little forced.

"I think we've gotten spoiled this last week, huh? But I guess it's time real life intruded."

"Yeah, I guess so."

Another pause, then a small sigh. "It was, uh, weird last night. With you not being here."

Dave's hand tightened on the phone, his heart pausing for just a second. Was she trying to tell him something? Or was he reading too much into it? Before he could say anything, she laughed again, and whatever moment he had imagined being there passed.

"You get some sleep, Big Guy, and I'll call you tomorrow night. Sound good?"

"Uh, yeah. Sure. Tomorrow night." She didn't respond, and he realized she had already disconnected the call. He stared down at the blank screen then hooked the phone back in its clip before draining the beer.

"Fuck." He had no idea what that had been about it and he was too damn tired to try to figure it out. He tossed the empty bottle into the trash then walked back through the house, not even bothering to grab his bag before he went upstairs.

He needed sleep. Several hours of uninterrupted,

deep sleep. Maybe then his mind would be sharp enough to figure out what the hell was going on, figure out what the hell he had to do to get his life back.

Maybe even figure out where he wanted his life to go.

Chapter Twenty-Five

The streets of Baltimore stretched out below them, square blocks lining up in neat little rows. The blocks thinned out, turning to industry along the water to the south, or spreading into larger residential areas to the north. CC adjusted her sunglasses and looked to the right, following the harbor out to the Key Bridge, then further out to the bay. Tony maneuvered the helicopter toward the east, back to the barracks. CC pulled her gaze from the water, back down to the streets below them, her eyes scanning, always moving, always looking.

She much preferred viewing the streets from this angle, no doubt about it. She loved the way the neighborhoods were lined up, loved the way the city stretched out, turning into the county. The landscape changed so quickly, from urban to suburban, to rural country up north.

She turned her head to the left but couldn't quite see the rolling hills of the north county. Then she realized what she was doing and rolled her eyes, almost laughing.

Almost.

Tony looked over at her, his eyes hidden behind the mirrored lenses of his aviator sunglasses, but the question was no less clear on his face. He was silently asking her what she was doing. She waved her hand in his direction, brushing him off.

There was no way she was going to answer him, not up here where she had to shout, despite the headsets and microphones. She wasn't going to answer him when they got back to the barracks either, no matter how much he pestered her.

And he had been pestering her. A lot. Wanting to know what was wrong with her, why she was so quiet, what was going on.

Yeah, right. Like she was going to tell him that she was pretty sure she screwed everything up. She had a hard enough time admitting that to herself.

Because she hadn't seen Dave since he left her house for work Tuesday afternoon. Four days had gone by and she had barely spoken to him, each conversation strained, awkward. And every time it seemed like he was going to ask her what was wrong, every time it seemed like he was about to get serious about something, she brushed him off. Or worse, laughed, like everything was just one big happy picnic.

She did it because she told herself he needed the laughter, didn't need anything serious, not with everything else going on. He was worried about his sister, worried about getting another text message. Worried that he hadn't heard anything since that morning in the hospital.

Yeah, that's what she told herself. Because she was so mature and self-sacrificing that way. Of course she was.

She laughed to herself, an absolutely humorless sound. What she was, was miserable. She missed him, plain and simple. Missed his gruffness, missed his tenderness. Missed the contradiction of the man himself.

And she really missed having him beside her at night, missed waking up next to him in the morning. Bubby was right, she was an idiot. Worse, she was afraid her father was right, and that she was a coward.

Because only a coward would refuse to admit they loved someone.

But she wasn't sure what to do about it. No, actually, she was. She needed to call Dave, to talk to him. Tell him how she felt. But what if she was wrong, and he didn't feel the same way? He didn't need the distraction or the strain that would put on him.

Yeah, she could pretty much talk herself out of anything if she wanted to. She was doing just that right now.

"Calling Carolann Covey. Reality to Carolann Covey. Come in."

"What?" Annoyance was clear in her voice as she turned toward Tony. He looked at her then nodded out the windshield, and she realized they were back at the barracks, that they had landed already.

"Yeah, okay." And she was never going to live this one down. She yanked off her headset and undid her harness as Tony powered the helicopter down. They ran through systems checks, pulled equipment and paperwork, got everything prepared for the next flight.

Then she grabbed her clipboard and made a beeline for the office, hoping to avoid any questions. Tony's laughter followed her, letting her know she couldn't avoid him forever.

She grabbed a bottle of water from the refrigerator then sat at the table, trying to focus on the reports in front of her. Which was pretty much like trying to get a two-year-old to sit still at a ballet. On her best days, she had trouble with reports. What made her think she'd actually be able to focus on them now?

Maybe she should call Dave now, ask him to meet later. Better yet, ask him to come over for dinner. They could throw some steaks on the grill, have some wine. Make up for four lost days of cuddle time.

Or maybe they could talk, and she could tell him how she really felt.

Making up for cuddle time sounded more promising.

For any of that to happen, though, she actually had to call him, not just sit there and think about calling him.

"I don't know whether to laugh at you, or smack you upside the head."

"What?" CC turned around, frowning as Tony walked into the room. He tossed her utility bag on the table in front of her then straddled one of the chairs, resting his arms along the back.

"You are completely out of it, walking around in a daze. It makes me wonder if being lovesick is an actual illness."

She narrowed her eyes at him, then curled her lip for added effect. "Haha, very funny. Wrong, but funny."

"Yeah, okay. If you say so." He snagged her water and took a sip, grinning when she rolled her eyes at him. "So is it that paramedic you've been seeing?"

"Is what who? And you couldn't get your own

drink?" She grabbed the bottle out of his hand and made a show of wiping off the top.

"Is the object of this apparent lovesickness the paramedic you've been seeing?"

"I am not lovesick. I've just got a lot on my mind. And that's none of your business anyway."

"Yeah, if you say so."

"I say so." CC pushed her chair back with a squeak then stood up. "Now if you'll excuse me, I have to go make a call."

Tony's chuckle followed her from the room and she wished there was a door she could slam, just to let him know she wasn't amused. She walked into the radio room then reached into her pants pocket for her phone. Except her pocket was empty. She patted each pocket of her jumpsuit, then went through them one by one. No phone. Dammit. Just what she needed.

She walked back into the break room, looking around the table and counters, the chairs, everywhere she could think of. Then she grabbed her utility bag and started digging through that.

Still no phone.

"What'd you lose this time?"

"My stupid phone. Have you seen it?"

"No. When was the last time you had it?"

"I don't remember." CC closed her eyes, thinking. She had it yesterday evening when she talked to Dave, she knew that much. Had she used it since then? No, she didn't think so. "Last night. I think."

Tony turned back to his own reports, shrugging. "Maybe you left it home."

"No, I'm pretty sure I brought it with me. At least, I thought I did." She frowned, mentally reviewing her steps from last night and this morning. She remembered tossing the phone on table of the porch room after talking to Dave last night. Went inside to eat then read. Bedtime...had she remembered to grab it this morning? She couldn't remember. She wasn't tied to her phone like most people and she didn't have her life on it like a lot of people. But she still tried to have it with her whenever she left the house. Usually.

"CC, you have been so distracted lately, it wouldn't surprise me if you found the thing in the refrigerator."

"I haven't been that bad."

Tony looked up, both eyebrows arched in what was clearly disbelief. "Did you check the chopper? Maybe it fell out. Or maybe it's in your car. Or maybe you left it at the hospital. Don't you have one of those find-your-phone app things?"

"No, I don't." Because she generally didn't worry about it that much. If she lost it again, she lost it again. It wouldn't be the first time. But she really needed it right now. She looked around the room once more, frowning. "I'll go look outside. It has to be around here somewhere."

She started walking out again then stopped in front of the refrigerator. Tony laughed when she opened the door and looked inside, so she grabbed a bottle of water and gave him a dirty look. "I was not looking for my phone. I had to get some more water, since you contaminated mine."

"Uh-huh, sure you did."

CC ignored him then spent the next hour looking everywhere for the damn phone. Maybe Tony had a point. She had been distracted. Or maybe she had just left the stupid thing sitting on the table again.

She called the hospital but nothing had been turned in. Yes, they'd call her if they found it. The thought crossed her mind that maybe she lost it on the actual call, when she had been helping the medic crew package the patient for transport. If that was the case, she may as well just chalk it up as lost for good, because there was no telling where it could be by now.

Then she wondered if she should take this as a sign. The only reason she had been looking for it was to call Dave, to ask him to meet, to talk, to tell him how she felt. Maybe the universe was using her lost phone as a not-so-subtle smack to her head, letting her know that wasn't a good idea.

Or maybe she was just so afraid of having that particular conversation that she was desperate to latch onto any excuse to get out of it.

"Still no luck?"

"Nope." CC flopped back into the chair and pulled the reports closer to her, determined to at least start them before going home.

"Just call the phone company and report it lost, then swing by on your way home and get a new one."

"Yeah, maybe. I want to make sure I didn't leave it at home first." Because wouldn't that be just her luck? She'd spend the small fortune to replace the phone, only to find hers sitting on the table out back, right where she left it.

Tony didn't say anything, just went back to his magazine, leaving her to work on her reports.

And convince herself this really wasn't a sign to *not* call Dave and talk to him.

Chapter Twenty-Six

Dave stood under the spray of water, letting it pound against his skull, against his back. The heat felt good, seeping into his sore muscles, the steam seeping into his skin. But it wouldn't be enough to completely erase the stress and tension that had been knotting his body for the last week.

Hell, for the last month. No, the last nine months. The only thing that would be able to accomplish that was ending the nightmare that his life had become.

Except for whatever was going on with him and CC. He had no idea what the hell to do about that. How could he, when he wasn't even sure what the hell was going on?

An image of her smiling face, of her long hair tangled around his arms as he held her, came to mind. His body reacted swiftly, with no warning, immediately stiffening at the image. Dammit to hell. He ground his teeth and ignored his sudden raging hard-on, doing his best to push all images, all thoughts, of CC from his mind. He grabbed the all-in-one shower gel and squeezed some onto his head, then lathered quickly, washing and rinsing off.

He was going to Duffy's tonight. Alone. Meeting his shift, having a few drinks, listening to the band. Having fun.

Even if it killed him.

He stood under the spray, letting the water run over him until it turned cold. Then he stood under it a little longer, until the cold water became almost painful.

At least that was one problem taken care of.

He turned the water off then pulled back the shower curtain and reached for a towel. His cell phone beeped, the accompanying vibration sending it gliding across the counter, closer to the edge. He cursed and reached for it, damn near slipping and falling as he did.

He looked down at the screen and frowned when he saw a text message from CC, then almost didn't open it. Almost. He threw the damp towel over the hook then tapped the screen.

Want to meet later?

He frowned again, wondering why she was sending a text message instead of calling. Then he realized she was working, must be up in the air somewhere. Either that, or she didn't feel up to having another strained and awkward conversation. He didn't think he could blame her for that one, because neither did he.

Have plans already.

He sent the message then tossed the phone on the counter, already feeling like an ass. The message was short and curt, even for him. He looked at the phone, wondering if he should send another one, then shook his head and pulled on his jeans. So what if it was curt?

Their recent phone conversations had been pretty much the same way, despite CC's attempt at laughing.

At every damn thing.

He wasn't much in a laughing mood.

The phone beeped again, vibrating against the counter. He wanted to ignore it, almost did. But he couldn't quite stop himself from reaching for it, no matter how much he told himself not to.

Need to talk.

His gut twisted and he swallowed, trying to push away the apprehension, the dread, at those three words. Words nobody in any kind of relationship ever wanted to hear.

His thumb tapped out his reply, hit send. *About?*

Another minute went by, tense, drawn-out, before the phone beeped once more.

In person. Please?

He frowned at the 'please', then felt his gut twist even more. Yeah, whatever she wanted to talk about couldn't be good, not if she was saying please.

Yeah, sure. Where?

There. Let her try to read into that one.

Where we met first time.

What the hell? So now she wanted him to play guessing games? What the hell was that supposed to mean?

Well, asshole, it could only mean one of two places, he thought. And it was a good bet she didn't mean an off-road trail in the middle of nowhere. He glanced at his watch, frowning, irritated at CC, irritated at himself. It was almost five thirty now. Even if he left right this minute, he'd still be sitting in traffic, despite it being a weekend.

Yeah, sure. An hour?

7:00

He shook his head, still not believing this is what they had been reduced to. And why? That was the million-dollar question. Apparently he'd be getting the answer tonight.

Sure. See you then.

He was ready to toss the phone back on the counter when it beeped one last time.

Thx Big Guy.

And Christ, why did part of him want to smile at the nickname? Why did part of him want to believe that whatever she wanted to talk about, it didn't involve calling it quits? Whatever they had going on, whatever they wanted to call it. Maybe she just wanted to talk, try to work things out, get rid of this damned awkwardness that had suddenly popped up between them.

Yeah. Or maybe she just wanted to call it quits, and wanted to tell him to his face instead of over the phone. Well, if that was the case, he had to at least give her credit for that much.

But if that was the case, would she have called him Big Guy?

Who the hell knew? And it didn't do a damn bit of good to speculate, not when he'd find out soon enough.

**

CC shrugged out of the flight suit and tossed it on the bed, then immediately grabbed a pair of jeans and a sweatshirt. She was tired, a headache was starting at the base of her skull, and all she wanted to do was sit out on the porch with a glass of wine.

She refused to allow the mental image of Dave sitting next to her form in her mind. Not just now, not until they talked. Because yeah, she had decided she needed to talk to him, tell him how she felt.

Apologize for being a crazy ass the last few days.

But first she had to run out to the phone store and get a new phone, because she still couldn't find hers. It wasn't on the table where she tossed it last night, wasn't in her car or on the kitchen counter or even in the pocket of her sweatpants. She just hoped to hell the store didn't close early on the weekend.

The phone in the kitchen rang, the shrill noise startling her because she wasn't used to the sound. Probably because she never used it. Never. Didn't even know why she was still paying for it.

She muttered under her breath and walked out to the kitchen, answering it on the fourth annoying ring. "Yeah?"

"Why aren't you answering your phone?"

CC pulled the phone away from her face and stared down at it, frowning. She moved it back to her ear and sighed, letting Bubby know she wasn't amused. "Uh, I am answering it. That's why I am now talking to you."

"Your cell phone, CC."

"Oh. Probably because I lost it again."

There was a long pause. Too long. She pulled the phone away again and stared at it, wondering if her brother was having a meltdown because he hadn't been able to reach her.

"What do you mean, you lost it?"

"Just what I said. I can't find it. I'm heading out now to get a new one. I'll call you back—"

"When did you have it last?"

244

"Bubby, not now. I'm not in a good mood and I don't need a lecture on losing things."

"CC, shut up and answer. When did you have it last?"

She rolled her eyes and walked over to the refrigerator, searching for something quick to snack on. If Bubby was going to lecture her, she wanted something in her stomach first. "Last night. I think. Maybe today but I don't remember grabbing it this morning. I probably lost it on a call this afternoon or something."

Her hand closed around a container of yogurt, stopped, then moved to the bag of chocolates instead.

"Fuck."

"Bubby, it's not like I haven't lost my phone before. It's not that big a deal."

"You sent Dave some text messages over an hour ago."

"No, I didn't." She was just about to pop a chocolate in her mouth then stopped, her eyes narrowing. "Oh my God, you cloned his phone! That's why you took it when we were at the hospital. Bubby, I can't believe you did that—"

"CC, did you not hear what I said? You sent Dave some text messages over an hour ago, asking him to meet you."

"And I said no, I didn't." His words finally sunk in, and the breath left her in a rush. Her hand tightened around the phone and she reached for the counter, grabbing it so she didn't fall. "Oh my God, he has my phone. The son of a bitch has my phone. Bubby, you need to call him, you need to tell Dave—"

"His phone is shut off. We completely lost him. We lost your phone as well."

"What? Oh God, Bubby—"

"CC, not now." His voice was cool, the words sharp and precise, irrationally calming her. "I need to know where you two first met."

She closed her eyes, took a deep breath. "Uh, on a call. Up north past Hereford, an ATV accident."

"Shit. That can't be right. CC, think. The message said 'where we met first time'. Where would that be?"

"His house. No. Ice cream. We met for ice cream." She took another deep breath, let it out. "The Thunderbird, on Old Eastern Avenue."

She pushed away from the counter, surprised her legs didn't give out under her, and hurried back to her room. She dragged her motorcycle boots from the closet and pushed her feet into them. Her hand was shaking so bad, she had trouble getting them zipped.

"We're on our way. CC, listen to me. Do not do anything stupid, do you hear me? You cannot go blazing in there. Do you understand me?"

"What time?" She yanked at the nightstand drawer, pulled it open and reached for her gun.

"Seven o'clock."

CC looked down at her watch, felt icy fear grip her. Fifteen minutes. It normally took her twenty-five to make the ride. She hurried back through the house, grabbing the keys to her motorcycle and her leather jacket. "Just get there, Bubby. You hear me? You don't let anything happen to him. I'm on my way."

"Dammit, CC, did you hear me? Do not go blazing in there."

"I'm leaving, Bubby." She was ready to throw the phone down, ready to just tear through the door and do exactly what her brother warned her not to do. But he called her name again, his voice firm, commanding.

"CC. He called him 'Big Guy'. Whoever he is, his last message said 'Thanks Big Guy'."

CC swallowed the cry of desperation bubbling in her throat, understanding the implication immediately. Only she called Dave that, and it was the one thing guaranteed to get his guard down.

She dropped the phone and ran out the door.

Chapter Twenty-Seven

Dave backed into the parking spot and cut the lights, looking around. The lot wasn't nearly as crowded as the first time he'd been here and he figured the handful of cars must belong to die hard ice cream fans.

There was no sign of CC's car, and he doubted if she'd be on the motorcycle. Then again, maybe not. The woman didn't seem to have a problem with cold, and it really wasn't that bad out.

He glanced down at his watch then climbed out of the car, muttering under his breath when his knee banged against the steering wheel. It was just a couple minutes till seven. He'd have a seat at one of the tables and wait, in case she was running late. He'd give her fifteen minutes, then leave.

Who was he kidding? He'd probably hang around for an hour, if for no other reason than wanting to get to the bottom of whatever was going on. And it wasn't like he could call her, not with his phone battery dead. And, of course, his car charger was right where he left it: in his truck. In South Carolina.

He just wanted his life to return to normal. Was that too much to ask? There was room there for CC—if she wanted. And yes, he hoped she wanted. Hoped he could figure out what they were doing tonight.

Gravel crunched under his feet as he walked through the parking lot, the lights throwing harsh circles here and there. Music drifted from the speakers at the front of the building, the annoying sound of the hip-hop-techno-pop mix grating on his nerves. The music was perfect for the few young people gathered around, though.

When the hell had he started feeling so old?

He glanced around, his eyes brushing over the small crowd. One teenage couple, paying more attention to each other than their ice cream. Another teenage couple, the tension so heavy between them, it was obvious they were minutes away from some kind of argument. A young family, the mom busy wiping melted chocolate from a squirming toddler's mouth as the dad cleaned up their trash. Another teen, sitting at a table by himself, using a knife to slice an apple then dip into it a cup of caramel sauce. Dave shook his head, figuring the kid was going to end up slicing himself, the way his hands were shaking so bad.

He looked closer as he walked by, saw the kid glance up at him with a frown. Not a kid. Technically. No, he was probably closer to nineteen, maybe twenty. And riding high on something, from the looks of him.

Dave kept walking, his eyes on the empty table furthest away from everyone. He didn't know how long it would take CC to get here, didn't know if the place would get more crowded or not. But he wanted privacy for when she did show up. For when they talked about whatever she wanted to talk about.

The metal chair squeaked as he lowered himself into it, squeaked again as he shifted, trying to get comfortable. He glanced down at his watch again.

7:02

A toddler's cry pulled his attention and he looked up, saw the family gathering their things to leave, much to the dismay of the kid. He arched his back and let out a wail, the screech drowning out the music.

Dave winced and figured he'd rather have the music.

The kid's scream must have been a signal of some kind because the two teenagers he had noticed earlier started arguing, their words loud but not loud enough he could make them out. Apple Guy stopped peeling long enough to look after the departing family, a frown on his face.

Dave looked over at the other couple and figured nothing would get their attention, not the way they were still staring at each other.

The kid's screams faded and Dave figured the parents had finally put him in the car and shut the door. He didn't envy them their ride home.

A shadow entered his line of vision from the right and he looked over to see someone walking toward him. Another kid, late teens, maybe early twenties, dressed in baggy jeans and a long sleeve shirt. He wore an apron smeared with melted ice cream and sauce, a frown on his face as he approached Dave's table.

"Tables are for patrons only. You need to order something."

"I'm waiting for someone."

"You need to order something."

Dave bit his tongue, telling himself to just go order

something, when he heard the low roar of a motorcycle flying toward them. He looked past the impatient kid, ignoring him as CC slid into the parking lot, the bike so low into the turn he worried she would lay it down, right there in front of him. His jaw clenched as a knot tightened in his gut and he had to force himself not to fly out of the chair and run over to her, yelling at her for doing something so foolish.

Apple Kid and Ice Cream Kid both turned to look at her, too, which was enough to assure him he wasn't overreacting. Then Ice Cream Kid turned back, still frowning.

"You need to order something."

"Yeah, I got it. No problem. She's here now, we'll be over in a minute." The kid frowned at him one more time then walked away, his gait slow, unhurried. Dave shook his head then stood up, planning on meeting CC half-way so they could order their damned ice cream and get this over with.

Right after he gave her a piece of his mind for that stunt she just pulled.

He watched as she pulled off her helmet and tossed it to the side, not bothering to stop when it rolled off the seat and landed in the gravel lot. Her expression was fierce, determined. Almost panicked. She hurried across the lot, her steps deliberate, quick.

What the hell? Why was she so pissed off?

Apple Kid stood up, knocking over the cup of caramel sauce with his elbow. Dave glanced at him, wondering what the hell was going on, then looked back at CC. Her hand reached inside her jacket as she moved closer, almost parallel to Ice Cream Kid, who was watching her with the same intensity as Apple Kid.

What the hell was going on?

Fear and certainty gripped him as realization suddenly blindsided him. "CC, no!"

He moved toward her, his hand outstretched, his eyes focused on Apple Kid. On the steady hand that was reaching behind his back.

"I know what you did."

The words shot through the night, clear, loud, drowning out the music. But something was wrong. Dave heard the words, but Apple Kid's mouth hadn't moved. He turned and felt the world drop from under his feet.

Ice Cream Kid held CC in front of him, one arm locked around her throat, tilting her head back. Light glinted off the blade pressed against the soft flesh of her neck, dangerously close to her carotid artery.

"Son of a bitch. Fuck." CC's soft words reached him over the screams of surprise, over the loud music and rush of footsteps. The two other couples were scrambling, running toward the parking lot. A van pulled in, tires kicking up gravel as it slammed to a stop, the passenger door flying open as Rob jumped out.

Dave looked over, saw Apple Kid crouched low in a typical shooter's stance, a pistol aimed at Ice Cream Kid.

At CC.

Everything happened in a split-second, the time it took for paralysis to seize him, the time it took for him to shake it off.

His eyes locked on CC's clear hazel gaze, filled with determination, regret, anger. But not fear. Love? He couldn't tell, couldn't think about that now, could only focus on the blade against her throat, steady, unwavering. He looked up then focused on the man—the kid—holding her.

Dave took a step closer, his hands held out to his side. Noise came from inside, a crashing sound that made Ice Cream Kid flinch. Dave swallowed when he saw the pinprick of blood well at the point of the knife.

The music stopped, cut off mid-wail, plunging them into silence.

"Let her go."

"No." The kid shook his head, the Adam's apple bobbing in his throat as he swallowed. "No. You need to know what it's like. You need to know how it feels to suffer because of what you did."

"What did I do?"

"You killed my brother."

Chapter Twenty-Eight

CC heard the words, desperate and raspy against her ear. She couldn't see the face of the guy holding her but she could see Dave's reaction. His body stiffened, tensed at the accusation. A muscle jumped in his tight jaw and his eyes narrowed a fraction of an inch. His broad chest rose and fell with one deep breath but he didn't move.

CC looked past Dave to the kid standing just behind him, crouched, a .44 held between two steady hands, pointing right at them. Yeah, probably not a kid. Probably a friend of Bubby's.

She hoped to hell he didn't have a twitchy finger.

And where the hell was Bubby? She sensed movement to her right but couldn't turn her head. She didn't need to, trusted her senses that he was there. And somebody else was there, too, whoever had gone inside to yank the plug on the music. That made three against one, four if you counted Dave.

Five if she counted herself.

The odds would be better if she could count

herself. She thought that might be a little too optimistic, considering she was standing there with a knife held to her throat. So yeah, she didn't have as much faith in three-to-one as she'd normally have, not with that sharp blade pressed against her skin.

"I didn't kill anyone."

CC slid her gaze back to Dave, watching, waiting. She had no idea what he was doing, what any of them were doing. She only knew that the guy holding her was rattled. His heart beat fast and crazy against her back, his breathing harsh in her ear. He adjusted his grip around her throat and stepped backward, pulling her with him.

"You did. Over there. You could have saved him but you didn't. You killed him."

"Tell me his name."

"You should know his name!"

CC flinched as the blade nicked her again, felt the itch of a tiny drop of blood against her skin. She kept her eyes on Dave, knowing he saw it, knowing that rage swept through him at the sight. But he looked calm, controlled as he kept his eyes on the guy behind her.

"Tell me his name."

The guy blew out a harsh breath, took another step back. Was he trying to get the wall right behind him? God, she hoped so.

"Keith. Keith Weber."

Dave's eyes remained blank, no spark of recognition flashing in the dark depths. He took another step forward, just a small one. CC heard a whispered caution to her right, recognized the voice as Bubby's.

"I remember Keith. He was a good guy."

"Then why did you let him die?"

"I didn't. There wasn't anything I could do for him." CC saw the stark truth of those words in his eyes, heard the regret in the slight tremor of his voice. He didn't know this guy's brother, had no idea who he was, but his words were still true. Hadn't he told her as much before? Hadn't he talked about the guilt he carried, knowing there were so many he couldn't help?

"No. You could have saved him, but you didn't. You let him die."

"There was nothing I could do." Dave moved forward again, just another inch. CC flinched again as the guy took another step back. Her hand reached up instinctively, ready to grab his arm, but she stopped, let it drop. Not yet.

"Yes, there was. You're a medic, you're supposed to save people." The guy's voice rose, almost desperate. CC closed her eyes, trying to visualize where they were, how close to the wall. A foot? An inch?

"I can't save everyone. Nobody can. I did my best."

"Your best wasn't good enough!"

"Don't you think I know that? Don't you think I live with that every day when I look in the mirror?" Dave shouted, frustration and regret in his voice. She looked at him, narrowing her eyes at him, willing him to look at her, if only for a split second. That was all she needed, for him to look at her, just for a second, just to let him know it wasn't true.

She sensed tension coming from her right, sensed the subtle change in the guy slightly behind Dave. But she couldn't worry about that, could only worry about Dave.

C'mon, Big Guy, look at me. Look at me.

And he did. Just for that quick split-second, faster

than the beat of a heart. Dave's shoulders relaxed, just a fraction of an inch as he inhaled deeply, let it out.

And moved forward another inch.

The guy moved back, and CC moved with him. He stopped, bumped against her just the slightest bit. Yes, the wall was behind him now. She took a shallow breath, waiting.

"Your brother. Keith. He wouldn't want you to do this." Dave's voice was calm, relaxed.

"No. No. It doesn't matter, you killed him. And now you need to know what it feels like to lose someone you care about." CC saw Dave's mouth open in denial, felt the guy behind her tense, felt his grip tighten around the handle of the blade.

And she made her move.

**

Dave opened his mouth, shouted, afraid to move but moving anyway, afraid he wouldn't be able to reach CC. His mind was blank, icy fear gripping him as he moved. He wouldn't be able to reach her in time. Nobody would be able to reach her in time.

Movement erupted around him, all at once but not at all, like frames from a video, clicking one at a time in front of him.

Rob, running forward, one agonizing step at a time. His hand outstretched, palm out, yelling.

Apple Kid, straightening, his gun coming up, his finger moving on the trigger.

CC, grim determination on her face as she reached up with both hands, closing around Ice Cream Kid's wrist, twisting. CC, her blonde ponytail swinging over shoulder as she threw her head back, hitting him in the face, using her body as leverage against his own, now pinned to the wall.

Then Dave was beside her, holding her, not knowing why they were on the ground, only knowing that CC was in his arms.

Alive.

He glanced over his shoulder, saw Rob and Apple Kid on top of Ice Cream Kid, saw another guy come running around the side of the building. He heard the thud of flesh against flesh, heard shouts and the wail of a siren in the distance but didn't care.

CC was in his arms, alive. His chest tightened, his heart squeezing painfully at the sight of blood on her neck. The breath left his lungs in a rush and he grabbed the hem of his shirt, yanking, trying to hold the material against her neck, not understanding why she was pushing at him.

"Big Guy, I'm okay, it's just a scratch. Let me up." She repeated the words several times, her voice softer and more reassuring each time until they finally sunk in. Dave gulped in air, huge lungsful, then slowly eased his hold on her.

CC twisted, pushing up onto her knees, her hands tight around his arms. Hair had fallen from her ponytail and hung around her shoulders, a few strands clinging to her flushed cheeks. Her hazel eyes were wide, staring into his. He dropped his gaze to her neck, felt bile sour in his stomach at the streaks of blood against the fragile skin of her throat. He sat back on his heels, forcing air into his lungs, wondering if he'd ever breathe normally again, wondering if his heart would ever slow down.

Then he grabbed CC and crushed her to him, just holding her, feeling her warm body against his. "Fuck. Shit. Don't ever do that again. Never. Do you understand? Never."

Her arms tightened around his waist as a small tremor went through her, barely noticeable. She leaned her head against his shoulder, her breath warm and reassuring against his neck. "Not like I did it on purpose."

"Why did you do it? What the hell were you thinking?" Dave still didn't know exactly what happened, figured he'd learn the details later. But he had pieced enough together to know that CC must have known something was happening and had come to warn him.

And damn near gotten herself killed instead.

She hadn't answered yet, so he repeated the question. "What the hell were you thinking?"

"I wasn't thinking. People in love tend to do that."

"What?" Dave pulled back, frowning, certain he hadn't heard correctly. "What did you say?"

"I said people in love don't think. I'm trying to tell you I love you. You could look a little happier about it, Big Guy."

"You—? Fuck. I thought you were getting ready to tell me to get lost."

CC shook her head. "I didn't send those messages, he did." Then she blinked, looked away, looked back at him, her teeth pulling on her lower lip. She looked suddenly lost, worried, like she wasn't sure what to do.

Dave cupped her face in his hands and pressed his mouth against hers, hard, fast, possessing. Then he pulled away, his gaze fierce. "I love you. And don't ever, ever, do that again. Ever. I can't go through that again."

She smiled, the expression warming him, so bright and promising.

So out of place.

But he didn't care and leaned forward to kiss her again, needing to touch her, taste her, prove to himself that she really was fine. Someone cleared their throat above and behind him, forcefully, stopping him.

"Yeah. Great. Glad you two got that worked out. But I really need you both standing right now, and not saying a word."

Dave looked over at Rob, noticed him standing over the unconscious Ice Cream Kid, a scowl on his face. He stood up, pulling CC with him, keeping his arm tight around her shoulder. He looked around, noticed the other two men were gone, as well as the van.

"Neither of you saw anyone else, got it? Not a word."

"Bubby—"

"Not a word, CC. I need you to trust me on this one."

Sirens screamed in the night as two police cars pulled into the parking lot, flashing blue lights casting rotating shadows over everything. Rob looked at both of them, then slowly raised his hands and nodded at them to do the same.

"What the fuck?" Dave caught the shake of CC's head as she raised her arms, bringing them up until she locked her fingers behind her head. He slowly did the same, not understanding what was going on.

Not until the cops threw open the doors and took cover behind them, their guns drawn. Of course they would, especially if they had been told there was a suspect with a gun, a suspect with a knife.

"I'm Trooper First Class Carolann Covey." CC's voice rang loud and clear in the night, startling Dave.

"My badge is in my back pocket, and I have a weapon in a shoulder holster. Your suspect is handcuffed on the ground."

Dave looked out of the corner of his eye, watched as one officer cautiously made his way toward them, gun drawn, the other officers covering him. He glanced over at Rob, saw his lips twitch in what might have been a grin, and realized the man was actually enjoying this. He looked over at CC, surprised at the bright smile on her face. Fuck. She was enjoying this, too.

Then she winked at him.

"Never a dull moment with me around, is there, Big Guy?"

Chapter Twenty-Nine

Once again, Dave was thankful that he was a paramedic and not a cop. Not if tonight was any indication of what they had to go through. Yeah, he understood everyone being taken in, understood everyone being questioned.

What he didn't understand was why it took more than five hours. And he had a feeling it would have taken much longer if CC wasn't a cop and if Rob wasn't whatever the hell he was. Because he was pretty sure he was a lot more than just a regular FBI agent.

He lifted the glass to his mouth and took a sip of bourbon, watching Rob. The three of them were back at CC's house She had pulled the bottle out from the back of a cabinet, loudly declaring they all needed it.

She didn't get any arguments from them.

CC was now tucked against his side, her legs curled under her as they sat on the loveseat on the back porch. The night air was chilly but not uncomfortable. Not with CC beside him.

He frowned, his thumb rubbing against the small

white bandage on her neck. Yes, it was only a scratch, but it could have been so much worse. And he never wanted to go through anything like that again, never wanted to feel like the world was being pulled out from under him. Because that's what it had felt like, when he saw Ice Cream Kid move, saw the blade of the knife shift, aiming for the pulse beat in CC's neck.

He gripped the glass tighter, afraid it would drop from his shaking hand. CC shifted, looked up at him with those beautiful eyes and smiled.

"I'm fine. Stop worrying."

"I know." He didn't say anything else, didn't tell her it would take some time before he stopped worrying. If he ever did.

Rob drained the last swallow from his glass then leaned forward and placed it on the table with a small clunk. He leaned back in the chair, his eyes resting briefly on his phone before he looked back at them.

"I have more information if you want it."

"Well that's about a stupid thing to say. Of course we want it." CC looked back at him, one brow raised in question. "We do want it, right?"

"Yeah." Dave nodded, looked back at Rob. "I'd like to know why."

"We may never know the answer to that, but here's what we do know. 'Ice Cream Kid'," Rob paused and looked at Dave, a small grin on his face. CC giggled and he tightened his arm around her.

"What? I didn't know what else to call him, alright?"

"Yes, well, 'Ice Cream Kid' is actually Seth Weber, 23 years old. He's had run-ins with the police before, mostly minor stuff. A history of mental illness. Turns out, he didn't even work at the ice cream parlor."

"Mental illness?"

"Yeah. We're still looking deeper on that one."

"And his brother?" Dave kept his gaze steady, not looking away, meeting Rob's serious eyes straight on. He held his breath, waiting.

"Keith Weber died in Iraq six years ago. You would have never met him."

Dave closed his eyes, some of the tension leaving him. Some, not all. "Doesn't mean there weren't others. Doesn't mean—"

"No. Stop, right now." CC shifted, coming up on her knees and forcing his face to hers. Her brows were lowered over her eyes, her expression serious as she held his face in her hands. "You don't get to say that. You don't get to second-guess yourself. You did the best you could, each time, and I'm not going to let you beat yourself up and wonder just because this guy fixated on you for some reason. Is that clear?"

She was serious, almost ferocious in her intensity, and Dave realized that he always wanted her on his side. No matter what. With CC by his side, they'd make one hell of a team.

He leaned forward and kissed her, just a brief press of his lips to hers, then pulled away. "Yes, ma'am."

"Good." She nodded, just in case he didn't understand, then curled back against his side, frowning at Rob.

"I don't get it. The way the guy was talking, it sounded like his brother had died recently. Certainly not six years ago."

Rob shrugged. "I don't know. It could be the illness, the lack of medication. It could be a lot of things. The only thing we know for sure is that he was in and out of the hospital until he turned eighteen. His brother was supposed to take care of him, but with him gone, there was nobody else. They released him onto the street, end of story. It looks like he's been staying in a cheap motel the last few months but they still have a lot to sort through before putting everything together."

"What happens to him now?"

"Well, he'll be charged, but probably never see a court room, not with his medical history. And hopefully he'll get some help. It's hard to say."

Dave thought he'd be angry at that answer, especially after what he'd done to CC. To Angie. But he wasn't. He didn't understand it, didn't condone it. But he wouldn't wish for the guy to have the book thrown at him and rot in jail for the rest of his life. He just hoped that he'd get the help he needed.

"So why me then? Why the fixation? How'd he even know who I was? Where to find me and get my number?"

"Your guess is as good as mine. They're looking through his computer, trying to track his moves, but it could be awhile before they know—if they ever do. He could have seen you somewhere, run into you on a call or at the hospital. Hell, even the grocery store. It's hard to say. I'm not even sure he could answer that question right now, if you asked him." Rob studied him for a second. "You okay with that?"

"I guess I have to be." He paused, thinking. "Yeah, I am. For now."

"Don't worry, Big Guy, I'll protect you."

"Which brings me to the next thing. You!" Rob shouted, causing CC and him both to jump. "I thought I told you not to go running in there, blazing. Isn't that what I said?"

"Yeah, but—"

"No buts. You damn near gave Dave and me both heart failure. You could have gotten yourself killed. What the hell were you thinking, running in like that without looking at your surroundings?"

"I *was* looking. Just at the wrong guy. I thought your buddy was the one I needed to watch out for."

"Apple Kid. Yeah, I thought the same thing at first."

"Apple Kid? Really?" The corners of Rob's mouth twitched and he shook his head.

"He looked like some strung out kid, sitting there peeling that damn apple. I didn't know what to think at first. And then when the other kid grabbed CC..." His voice drifted off, the words fading as remembered fear went through Dave. He swallowed against it and took a deep breath. He didn't think he could ever go through that again, never wanted to.

Rob glanced down at his phone, frowned, then stood up. "Well maybe you'll have better luck getting through to her. She's all yours now, and you're welcome to her with my blessings."

CC swung her legs down, staring up at her brother. "Where are you going?"

"Me? I'm going home."

"Home? As in back home, to South Carolina?"

"That is where I live, CC."

"Now? But it's late! Why don't you stay, leave in the morning?"

"Here, with you two? Uh, no, I'll pass. Besides, my ride's waiting, and I still have my own reports to do."

CC stood the same time Dave did, then moved toward her brother, stopping him with a hand on his arm, frowning. Something passed between them, something Dave didn't understand. "Bubby, are you going to be okay? I mean, with everything—you're not going to be in any trouble, are you?"

"Nothing I can't handle, don't worry." He leaned down and hugged his sister, pulling her in tight, and Dave saw a glimpse of emotion on the man's face for the first time that night. Raw, real. Anguished. But the glimpse was gone in a second, replaced by Rob's normal relaxed expression.

"Thank you, Bubby. For everything."

"Hey, that's what family does, right?" He squeezed her one more time, then let her go, turning to Dave. He put his hand out, but instead of Rob accepting it, the man pulled him into a quick bro hug, shoulder-to-shoulder, patting him on the back. "Just remember, I know where to find you."

Dave laughed, not entirely certain the man was joking, then followed them back into the house, waiting while CC said goodbye again at the door. He heard the door close, heard the click of the lock as she turned it. Then she was back in the living room, standing in front of him.

Alive. So very alive.

He pulled her into his arms and kissed her, his mouth hot, demanding, surrendering. Never wanting to let go, needing. Now. He grabbed her shirt and pulled it over her head, threw it behind him as he started walking, guiding her backward, heading for her room. She laughed, tugged at his own shirt, then stopped, her palm warm and steady in the middle of his chest, covering his heart. He placed his hand over hers, gently squeezing her fingers, waiting for her to look up at him.

"I love you CC. And if you ever scare me like that again, I'll—I don't know what I'd do, so just don't."

"Scared *you?* You're not the only one who was scared. When Bubby called me—" She shook her head and swallowed, blinking. "I was pissed."

"Pissed? Why on earth were you pissed?"

"Because I had been planning all day on figuring out how to tell you I loved you, then I find out some jerk has different plans. So yeah, I was pissed. So don't you ever do anything like that again."

Dave laughed, a real laugh that eased some of the tension, some of the fear that still gripped him. He leaned down and kissed her, hard and quick. "Maybe next time we each have something important to say to the other, we just do it like normal people."

"Normal?" Mock horror lit her face. "Where's the fun in that?"

"Fun? I don't know how much more fun I can handle."

"Really? That's a shame." A glint lit her eyes, her mouth turning up in a sly, sexy smile. She wrapped her hand in the waistband of his jeans and walked backward, tugging him along. "Because I thought we could both use a little fun right now."

"Yeah? What'd you have in mind?"

"Well, you look a little tense. I thought a massage might help."

Dave grinned, thinking of their last massage. "I don't know, maybe. What else?"

"Well, then I was thinking we could have some ice cream." She pulled him into the bedroom, kept walking until her legs hit the edge of the mattress. Then she undid the snap and zipper of his jeans and pushed them down his hips, her mouth hot against his chest where she kissed him. "You know how much I like my ice cream. With hot fudge. And whip cream."

"Oh, God." He closed his eyes, enjoying her touch, her voice, everything about her. Then he let out a grunt of surprise as CC suddenly turned and pushed him, so he was sprawled out on the bed, looking up at her. She climbed on top, straddled his hips, and smiled.

"Then, after the ice cream, we'll probably need a shower. I have this nice new gel I want to try."

"You're killing me, CC."

"Hm." She lowered her head, his lips trailing from his neck, down across his chest, her tongue darting out and tracing the lines of his tattoo. "You'll have plenty of time to rest when we leave tomorrow."

His eyes shot open and he lifted his head, looking at her, at the playful grin on her face. "Leave tomorrow?"

"Yup."

"Uh, leave where? I work on Monday."

"Not anymore you don't. Apparently Bubby has a far reach." She grinned again, slid down his legs, tugging at his jeans. "Have I told you how much I love it when you go commando?"

His head fell back as her hand closed around him, stroking him. No, not yet. He reached down, grabbed her hand, pulled her up.

"CC." His voice was hoarse already, damn her. He cleared his throat, looked down at her. "Where are we going?"

"Back down to South Carolina. You didn't think I was going to let you out of taking me to Charleston that easily, did you?"

"But—"

"We're staying at my parents' house. For a week.

And our flight leaves in eight hours." She reached down, her hand closing over him again, stroking him. "Now, do you really want to talk about this right this minute?"

He growled and reached for her, rolling her over so he was on top. "Hell no. No, I have more important things to do. Like show you how much I love you."

"As long as I get a turn to show you how much I love you, I'm good with that." She pulled his head down to hers and kissed him, long, slow sweet.

And they did exactly that, until it was time to meet the plane.

And really, who cared if they were just a little late?

*****

BREAKING PROTOCOL

Lisa B. Kamps

ABOUT THE AUTHOR

Lisa B. Kamps is the author of the best-selling series The Baltimore Banners, featuring "hard-hitting, heart-melting hockey players", on and off the ice. BREAKING PROTOCOL is the third title of her new series, *Firehouse Fourteen*, featuring hot and heroic firefighters.

Lisa has always loved writing, even during her assorted careers: first as a firefighter with the Baltimore County Fire Department, then a very brief (and not very successful) stint at bartending in east Baltimore, and finally as the Director of Retail Operations for a busy Civil War non-profit.

Lisa currently lives in Maryland with her husband and two sons, one very spoiled Border Collie, two cats with major attitude, several head of cattle, and entirely too many chickens to count.

Interested in reaching out to Lisa? She'd love to hear from you, and there are several ways to contact her:

Website: www.LisaBKamps.com
Newsletter: www.lisabkamps.com/signup/
Email: LisaBKamps@gmail.com
Facebook: www.facebook.com/authorLisaBKamps
Twitter: twitter.com/LBKamps
Goodreads: www.goodreads.com/LBKamps
Instagram: www.instagram.com/lbkamps/

CROSSING THE LINE
The Baltimore Banners Book 1

Amber "AJ" Johnson is a freelance writer who has one chance of winning her dream-job as a full-time staffer: capture an interview with the very private goalie of Baltimore's hockey team, Alec Kolchak. But he's the one man who tries her patience, even as he brings to life a quiet passion she doesn't want to admit exists.

Alec has no desire to be interviewed--he never has, never will. But he finds himself a reluctant admirer of AJ's determination to get what she wants...and he certainly never counted on his attraction to her. In a fit of frustration, he accepts AJ's bet: if she can score just one goal on him in a practice shoot-out, he would not only agree to the interview, he would let her have full access to him for a month, 24/7.

It's a bet neither one of them wants to lose...and a bet neither one can afford to win. But when it comes time to take the shot, can either one of them cross the line?

Turn the page for an exciting peek at CROSSING THE LINE, available now.

Lisa B. Kamps

"Oh my God, what have I done?" AJ muttered the phrase under her breath for the hundredth time. She wanted to rub her chest but she couldn't reach it under the thick pads now covering her. She wanted to go home and curl up in a dark corner and forget about the whole thing.

Me and my bright ideas.

"Are you going to be okay?"

AJ snapped her head up and looked at Ian. The poor guy had been given the job of helping her get dressed in the pads, and she almost felt sorry for him. Almost. Between her nervousness and the threat of an impending migraine, she was too preoccupied to muster much sympathy for anyone else right now.

"Yeah, I'm fine." She took a deep breath and stood, wobbling for only a second on the skates. This was not how she had imagined the bet going. When she cooked up the stupid idea, she had figured on having a few days to at least practice.

Well, not really. If she was honest with herself, she never even imagined that Alec would agree to it. But if he had, then she would have had a few days to practice.

So much for her imagination.

She took another deep breath then followed Ian from the locker room. It didn't take too long for her gait to even out and she muttered a thankful prayer. She only hoped that she didn't sprawl face-first as soon as she stepped on the ice.

Her right hand clenched around the stick, getting used to the feel of it, getting used to the fit of the bulky glove—which was too big to begin with. This would have been so much easier if all she had to do was put on a pair of skates. She had never considered the possibility of having to put all the gear on, right down to the helmet that was a heavy weight bearing down on her head.

She really needed to do something with her imagination and its lack of thinking things all the way through.

AJ took another deep breath when they finally reached the ice. She reached out to open the door but was stopped by Ian.

"Listen, AJ, I'm not even going to pretend I know what's going on or why you think you can do this, but I'll give you some advice. Shoot fast and low, and aim for the five and two holes—those are Alec's weak spots. The five hole is—"

"Between the legs, I know." AJ winced at the sharpness of her voice. Ian was only trying to help her. He had no reason to realize she knew anything about ice hockey, and not just because she liked to write about it. She offered him a smile to take the bite from her words then slammed the butt of the stick down against the door latch so it would swing open. Two steps later and she was standing on a solid sheet of thick ice.

AJ breathed deeply several times then slowly made her way to the other side of the rink, where Alec was nonchalantly leaning against the top post of the net talking to Nathan. They both watched as she skated up to them and came to a smooth stop. Alec's face was expressionless as he studied her, and she wondered what thoughts were going through his mind. Probably nothing she really wanted to know.

Nathan nodded at her, offering a small smile. She had to give the guy some credit for not laughing in her face when she asked his opinion on her idea. "Well, at least it looks like you've been on skates before. That's a plus."

AJ didn't say anything, just absently nodded in his direction. The carefree attitude she had been aiming for was destroyed by the helmet sliding down over her forehead. She pushed it back on her head then glanced at the five pucks lined neatly on the goal line. All she had to do was get one of them across. Just one.

She didn't have a chance.

She pushed the pessimistic thought to the back of her mind. "So, do I get a chance to warm up or take a practice shot?"

Alec sized her up then briskly shook his head. "No."

AJ swallowed and glanced at the pucks, then back at Alec. "Alrighty then. A man of few words. That's what I like about you, Kolchak." AJ though he might have cracked a smile behind his mask but she couldn't be sure. She sighed and leaned on her stick, trying to look casual and hoping it didn't slip out from under her and send her sprawling. "So, what are the rules?"

"Simple. You get five chances to shoot. If you score, you win. If you don't, I win." Alec swept the pucks to the side with the blade of his stick so Nathan could pick them up. She followed the moves with her eyes and tried to ignore the pounding in her chest.

She had so much riding on this. Something told her that Alec was dead serious about being left alone if she lost. It had been a stupid idea, and she wondered if she would have had better luck at trying to wear him down the old-fashioned way.

She studied his posture and decided probably not. He had been mostly patient with her up to this point, but even she knew he would have reached his limit soon.

"All or nothing, then. Fair enough. So, are you ready?"

AJ didn't hear his response but thought it was probably something sarcastic. She sighed then turned to follow Nathan to the center line, her heart beating too fast as her feet glided across the ice. She shrugged her shoulders, trying to readjust the bulk of the pads, and watched as Nathan lined the pucks up.

He finished then straightened and faced her, an unreadable expression on his face. He finally grinned and shook his head.

"I have no idea if you know what you're doing or not, but good luck. You're going to need it."

"Gee, thanks."

Nathan walked across the ice to the bench and leaned against the outer boards, joining a few of the other players gathered there. AJ wished they were gone, that they had something better to do than stand around and watch her make a fool of herself.

Well, she had brought it on herself.

She closed her eyes and inhaled deeply, pushing everything from her mind except what she was about to do. When she opened her eyes again, her gaze was on the first puck. Heavy, solid...nothing more than a slab of black rubber...

Okay, so she wasn't going to have any luck becoming one with the puck. Stupid idea. AJ had never understood that whole Zen thing anyway.

She swallowed and began skating in small circles, testing her ankles as she turned first one way then another, testing the stick as she swept it back and forth across the ice in front of her. Not too bad. Maybe she hadn't forgotten—

"Sometime today would be nice!"

AJ winced at the sarcasm in Alec's voice and wished she had some kind of comeback for him. Instead she mumbled to herself and got into position behind the first puck. She didn't even look up to see if he was ready. Didn't ask if it was okay to start, she just pushed off hard and skated, the stick out in front of her.

This was her one shot, she couldn't blow it.

*****

Lisa B. Kamps

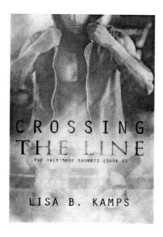

Amber "AJ" Johnson is a freelance writer who has her heart set on becoming a full-time sports reporter at her paper. She has one chance to prove herself: capture an interview with the very private goalie of Baltimore's hockey team, Alec Kolchak. But he's the one man who tries her patience, even as he brings to life a quiet passion she doesn't want to admit exists.

Alec has no desire to be interviewed--he never has, never will. But he finds himself a reluctant admirer of AJ's determination to get what she wants...and he certainly never counted on his attraction to her. In a fit of frustration, he accepts AJ's bet: if she can score just one goal on him in a practice shoot-out, he would not only agree to the interview, he would let her have full access to him for a month, 24/7.

It was a bet neither one of them wanted to lose...and a bet neither one could afford to win. But when it came time to take the shot, could either one of them cross the line?

Forensics accountant Bobbi Reeves is pulled back into a world of shadows in order to go undercover as a personal assistant with the Baltimore Banners. Her assignment: get close to defenseman Nikolai Petrovich and uncover the reason he's being extorted. But she doesn't expect the irrational attraction she feels—or the difficulty in helping someone who doesn't want it.

Nikolai Petrovich, a veteran defenseman for the Banners, has no need for a personal assistant—especially not one hired by the team. During the last eight years, he has learned to live simply...and alone. Experience has taught him that letting people close puts them in danger. He doesn't want a personal assistant, and he certainly doesn't need anyone prying into his personal life. But that doesn't stop his physical reaction to the unusual woman assigned to him.

They are drawn together in spite of their differences, and discover a heated passion that neither expected. But when the game is over, will the secrets they keep pull them closer together...or tear them apart?

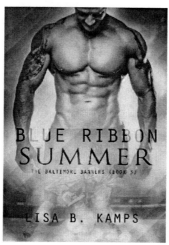

BLUE RIBBON
SUMMER
THE BALTIMORE BANNERS (BOOK 3)

LISA B. KAMPS

Kayli Evans lives a simple life, handling the daily operations of her small family farm and acting as the primary care-taker for her fourteen-year-old niece. She knows the importance of enjoying each minute, of living life to its fullest. But she still has worries: about her older brother's safety in the military, about the rift between her two brothers, and about her niece's security and making ends meet. And now there's a new worry she doesn't want: Ian Donovan, her brother's friend.

Ian is a carefree hockey player for the Baltimore Banners who has relatively few worries—until he finds himself suddenly babysitting his seven-year-old nieces for an extended period of time. He has no idea what he's doing, and is thrust even further into the unknown when he's forced to participate in the twins' newest hobby. Meeting Kayli opens a different world for him, a simpler world where family, trust, and love are what matters most.

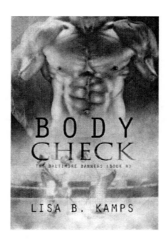

Baltimore Banners defenseman Randy Michaels has a reputation for hard-hitting, on and off the ice. But he's getting older, and his agent has warned that there are younger, less-expensive players who are eager to take his place on the team. Can his hare-brained idea of becoming a "respectable businessman" turn his reputation around, or has Randy's reputation really cost him the chance of having his contract renewed?

Alyssa Harris has one goal in mind: make the restaurant she's opened with her three friends a success. It's not going to be easy, not when the restaurant is a themed sports bar geared towards women. It's going to be even more difficult because their sole investor is Randy Michaels, her friend's drool-worthy brother who has his own ideas about what makes an interesting menu.

Will the mismatched pair be able to find a compromise as things heat up, both on and off the ice? Or will their differences result in a penalty that costs both of them the game?

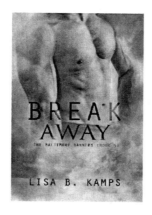

Jean-Pierre "JP" Larocque is a speed demon for the Baltimore Banners. He lives for speed off the ice, too, playing fast and loose with cars and women. But is he really a player, or is his carefree exterior nothing more than a show, hiding a lonely man filled with regret as he struggles to forget the only woman who mattered?

Emily Poole thought she knew what she wanted in life, but everything changed five years ago. Now she exists day by day, helping care for her niece after her sister's bitter divorce. It may not be how she envisioned her life, but she's happy. Or so she thinks, until JP re-enters her life. Now she realizes there's a lot more she wants, including a second chance with JP.

Can these two lost souls finally find forgiveness and Break Away to the future? Or will the shared tragedy of their past tear them apart for good this time?

Valerie Michaels knows all about life, responsibility--and hockey. After all, her brother is a defenseman for the Baltimore Banners. The last thing she needs--or wants--is to get tangled up with one of her brother's teammates. She doesn't have time, not when running The Maypole is her top priority. Could that be the reason she's suddenly drawn to the troubled Justin Tome? Or is it because she senses something deeper inside him, something she thinks she can fix?

On the surface, Justin Tome has it all: a successful career with the Banners, money, fame. But he's been on a downward spiral the last few months. He's become more withdrawn, his game has gone downhill, and he's been partying too much. He thinks it's nothing more than what's expected of him, nothing more than once again failing to meet expectations and never quite measuring up. Then he starts dating Val and realizes that maybe he has more to offer than he thinks.

Or does he? Sometimes voices from the past, voices you've heard all your life, are too strong to overcome. And when the unexpected happens, Justin is certain he's looking at a permanent Delay of Game--unless one strong woman can make him see that life is all about the future, not the past.

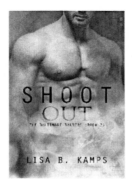

Sometimes it takes a sinner...

Nicole Taylor has been fighting to get on the right side of the tracks all her life, but never as hard as the last two years. Finally free from an abusive relationship, her focus is on looking forward. Her first step in that direction? A quick get-away to immerse herself in her photography--and a steamy encounter with a gorgeous green-eyed stranger.

To love a saint...

As a forward for The Baltimore Banners, shooting fast and scoring often is just part of the game for Mathias "Mat" Herron. Off the ice is a different story and this off-season, he has a different goal in mind: do whatever it takes to rid himself of the asinine nickname he was recently given by some of his teammates. An encounter with a beautiful stranger helps him do just that.

And life to teach them both what's important...

When reality collides with fantasy, will passion be enough to see them through? Or will it take a shoot-out of another kind to show them what matters most?

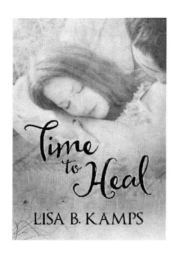

Jake Evans has been in the Marine Corps for seventeen years, juggling his conflicting duties to country and his teenage daughter. But when he suffers a serious injury and is sent home, he knows he'll be forced to make decisions he doesn't want to. Battered in spirit and afraid of what the future may hold, he takes the long way by driving cross-country.

He never expected to meet Alyce Marshall, a free-spirited woman on a self-declared adventure: she's running away from home.

In spite of her outward free spirit, Alyce has problems of her own she must face, including the ever-present shadow of her father and his influence on her growing up. She senses similarities in Jake, and decides that it's up to her to teach the tough Marine that life isn't just about rules and regulations. What she doesn't plan on is falling in love with him...and being forced to share her secret.

Michaela Donaldson had her whole life planned out: college, music, and a happy-ever-after with her first true love. One reckless night changed all that, setting Michaela on a new path. Gone are her dreams of pursuing music in college, replaced by what she thinks is a more rewarding life. She's a firefighter now, getting down and dirty while doing her job. So what if she's a little rough around the edges, a little too careless, a little too detached? She's happy, living life on her own terms--until Nicky Lansing shows back up.

Nick Lansing was the stereotypical leather-clad bad boy, needing nothing but his fast car, his guitar, his never-ending partying, and his long-time girlfriend--until one bad decision changed the course of two lives forever. He's on the straight-and-narrow now, living life as a respected teacher and doing his best to be a positive role model. Yes, he still has his music. But gone are his days of partying. And gone is the one girl who always held his heart. Or is she?

One freak accident brings these two opposites back together. Is ten years long enough to heal the physical and emotional wounds from the past? Can they reconcile who they were with who they've become--or will it be a case of Once Burned is enough?

Angie Warren was voted the Most Likely to Succeed in school. She was also voted the Most Responsible. And responsible she is: she made it through college on a scholarship and she's even working her way through Vet School. She has an overprotective older brother she adores and a part-time job tending bar that adds some enjoyment to her life. In fact, that's the only pleasure she has. She's bored and in desperate need of a change. Too bad the one guy she has her sights set on is the one guy completely off-limits.

Jay Moore knows all about excitement and wouldn't live life any other way. From his job as a firefighter to his many brief relationships, his whole life is nothing but one thrilling experience after the other. Except when Angie Warren enters the picture. He's known her for years and there is no way he's going to agree to give her the excitement she's looking for. Even Jay knows where to draw the line—and dating his friend's baby sister definitely crosses all of them.

Too bad Angie has other plans. But will either one of them remember that when you're Playing With Fire, someone is bound to get burned?

Dave Warren knows all about protocol. As a firefighter/paramedic, he has to. What he doesn't know is when his life became nothing more than routine, following the rules day in and day out. Has it always been that way, or was it a gradual change? Or did it have anything to do with his time spent overseas as a medic with the Army Reserves? He's not sure, but it's something he's learned to accept and live with—until a series of messages upsets his routine. And until one spitfire Flight Medic enters his life.

Carolann "CC" Covey has no patience for protocols. Yes, they're a necessary evil, a part of her job, but they don't rule her life. She can't let them—she knows life is for the living, a lesson learned the hard way overseas. Which is why her attraction to the serious and staid Dave Warren makes no sense. Is it just a case of "opposites attract", or is it something more? Will CC be able to teach him that sometimes rules need to be broken?

And when something sinister appears from Dave's past to threaten everything he's come to love, will he learn that Breaking Protocol may be the only way to save what's really important?

CPSIA information can be obtained at www.ICGtesting.com
Printed in the USA
LVOW11s1744200916

505434LV00001B/32/P